LILY COULDN'T STAND IT ANY LONGER

"Saundra, I'm sick of this. If you don't want to talk to me, don't talk to me. But please stop lying there like a dead kielbasa."

Saundra started whimpering. And Lily thought, Oh, no, she's crying again. Then Lily saw a smile on Saundra's face.

"What on earth is a dead kielbasa?"

Okay. A dead kielbasa is—"

Saundra smiled again. "Not that. I don't want to talk about that. I want to talk about me."

"What about you?" Lily asked. "What part of you do you want to talk about?"

"My heart. . . . It's broken."

It sounded so dramatic. A broken heart. Was it possible? Did such things really happen?

Bantam Starfire Books of related interest
Ask your bookseller for the books you have missed

Love's
Detective

by
J.D.
Landis

TORONTO • NEW YORK • LONDON • SYDNEY • AUCKLAND

RL 6, IL age 10 and up

LOVE'S DETECTIVE
A Bantam Book / December 1984

Starfire and accompanying logo of a stylized star are trademarks of Bantam Books, Inc.

ISBN 0-553-24529-5

Published simultaneously in the United States and Canada

Bantam Books are published by Bantam Books, Inc. Its trademark, consisting of the words "Bantam Books" and the portrayal of a rooster, is Registered in U.S. Patent and Trademark Office and in other countries. Marca Registrada. Bantam Books, Inc., 666 Fifth Avenue, New York, New York 10103.

PRINTED IN THE UNITED STATES OF AMERICA

O   0 9 8 7 6 5 4 3 2 1

For Sara and Becca and Cesca and Andrea

Contents

1

Hair

Lily Leonard wondered what was happening to her sister.

"What's the matter with you these days?" she asked when she finally got up the courage, after what seemed like weeks of watching Saundra jump for joy one minute, only to crumble the next.

"Who said anything was the matter?" Saundra snapped.

"You're not acting yourself these days."

"And what's myself? Who's myself? Where's myself?" Saundra rose on tiptoes as she spoke.

"You're my wonderful sister," Lily answered, hoping it would cover Saundra's strange list of questions.

"A lot of good that does me." Saundra glared at Lily with her beautiful gray eyes, then stuck her perfect little nose in the air, turned around on the toe of one foot, and left their bedroom, slamming the door behind her.

That hurt. Lily sat down on her bed. She knew that there had been a time when it had done Saundra no good to have her as a sister. It was as if she hadn't existed except as a curly-headed little big-mouth who made their parents exclaim how bright she was and who became Saundra's roommate against Saundra's will.

But then, last year, it had done Saundra a lot of good to have Lily as her sister in the battle against Meredith Meredith, Saundra's arch rival at the American Ballet Center.

These days, though, it wasn't doing Lily any good to have a sister who was going through something. Lily didn't know what it was, but whatever it was, it had changed Saundra in just a few weeks from a wonderful older sister to the kind of sister she used to be before Lily had helped her last year to win the audition against Meredith Meredith for a role in the second company of the American Ballet Center: haughty and secretive and distant and sometimes just plain mean.

Lily didn't know what was troubling Saundra. But whatever it was, she wanted it to go away. She wanted her almost perfect sister back, the one who'd become open and generous and helpful and kind and had even learned how to give Lily a kiss on the cheek without making both of them feel embarrassed and phony. In the last year they had been like best friends, except they were even closer because they were sisters. And the fact that Saundra was fifteen and Lily was ten didn't matter at all. Lily didn't know any best friends with that much difference in age between them. But age didn't mean much when you were sisters, not sisters like them: they were friends, they were relatives, they were each other's helpers and supporters and biggest fans.

Whenever the second company was performing, Lily would go to the theater with her father and mother and sit there and keep her eyes on Saundra alone, and every move that Saundra made on the stage, every step she took, every jump she jumped, every bend into which her body so gracefully flowed, was shared by Lily and made Lily's heart pound and her skin prickle with perspiration and, finally, her whole being open up with pride and joy in her sister's performance.

And Saundra was proud of Lily too. She not only gave Lily credit for having helped her win the audition, but she also admitted that in some ways Lily was both different and better than she was. "Lily is a real brain," Saundra would say. "Lily can think even better than I can dance. And dancing's very easy compared to thinking. When you dance, you dance, and everybody can see what you're doing. But when you think, only you know what you're thinking, and unless you can talk as well as you can think, people don't know *how* smart you are. And can Lily talk! Lily can talk even better than she can think, sometimes. She can think and she can talk, and not only that but she's got curly hair. Sometimes I think I would die for curly hair!"

Never mind Saundra's remarks about her thinking and her talking. What really got to Lily and made her feel great all over at the same time that it made her feel embarrassed, too, was what Saundra said about her hair. Saundra had the most beautiful hair in the world. It was long and black and shiny and, when she didn't wear it up for dancing, hung down her back like a mysterious curtain into a glamorous world. It never ceased to amaze Lily that Saundra liked her hair and was even jealous of it. It meant they were jealous of the same thing about one another, and no one thing about them could have been so different. Lily certainly didn't want to be Saundra, because Lily was still learning what she was herself, and the more she learned, the more she grew to like what she discovered. But she certainly wouldn't have minded having Saundra's hair. At least on a trial basis. Now and then she even imagined going into a wig store all by herself and trying on a long, black head of hair. But she knew she never would. What would be the use? Curly hair was *her* hair. She might as well learn to live with it. And it was certainly easier to live with it when her own gorgeous sister said how nice it was. Lily wasn't sure she believed Saundra when she said that. But it made her feel so good to hear it that she put her suspicions out of her mind and let herself be gloriously embarrassed.

Too bad they couldn't share their hair, Lily sometimes thought. But they couldn't. Besides, there were more important things to share. And right now the most important of all were the love and friendship they'd found over the past year but had somehow lost because something was happening to Saundra and she couldn't say what it was.

2
A
Deep,
Dark
Secret

Just when Lily was about to give up hope that Saundra would come back into their room and apologize, the door opened and Saundra walked in.

"You don't have to say anything," said Lily. "I forgive you."

"And I accept your apology." Saundra started to fling off her clothes.

"Wait a minute," said Lily.

Saundra laughed as she wiggled out of her skin-tight jeans.

"I didn't apologize," Lily said. "I just meant that *you* didn't have to."

"Thank goodness," said Saundra, peeling herself out of her leotard. "I have enough to feel guilty about."

"You do? What?"

"*This*." Saundra kicked her tiny French under-

5

pants off the end of her big toe, so they floated across the room like a lazy pink bird, and spread her arms wide so she stood naked right before Lily's eyes.

"I've seen it before," Lily said. "So you don't have to feel guilty about corrupting a minor."

"I'm corrupting myself," said Saundra with a strange smile. "And I feel great about it."

"I thought you felt guilty."

"I do. And it's great to feel guilty."

"It is?"

"About this it is."

"About your body?"

"About what my body does to other people."

"When you dance?" Lily asked, though the only guilt she could imagine Saundra feeling about dancing was the guilt of making people long to capture the kind of beauty that disappeared the moment it was born.

"I don't dance naked." Saundra giggled at the idea.

"Of course you don't. The only thing you do naked is take a shower."

"That's what you think," said Saundra.

"And get dressed, of course," said Lily.

"Guess again."

"Skinny-dip?"

"You know I don't go to the beach. I'm dancing all summer."

"But I thought you said you didn't dance naked."

"I don't," Saundra said, too cheerful to sound impatient. "I dream."

"But you wear a nightgown."

"I dream I'm naked," Saundra said, starting to dance around the room, not her usual classic ballet but some kind of modern thing, on her knees with her elbows trying to touch her shoulders and her back arched so tightly that bones showed through her skin like the fingers of a crowd of people trapped within her. "I dream I'm naked and the whole world is watching."

"How embarrassing," said Lily, who preferred to dream of new sweaters.

Saundra rolled onto her back and crossed one leg over the other. "Or only one person is watching."

"Who?"

"One person."

"I hope he doesn't have a camera," said Lily.

"He doesn't need a camera." Saundra crossed the other leg over the first one and hooked her ankles together. Her limbs were twisted. But she was graceful anyway. Her body could do no wrong.

"Why not?"

"His mind is his camera. My naked body is printed indelibly on the film of his consciousness."

"On the film of his consciousness? What does that mean?"

"He memorizes me. He consumes me. He drinks me in."

"What is he, a straw?"

"He's a prince," said Saundra, rising with her legs still crossed. "A god. He's invincible. Except when he sees my body. You should see what my body does to him."

"No thanks. But who is this prince guy, anyway?"

"You'll recognize him when you see what my

7

body does to him." Saundra hobbled cross-legged over to her closet. "And you ask me why I feel guilty!"

"Not anymore I don't."

"Why not?"

"Because I know why you feel guilty. You feel guilty because you're having bad dreams."

"Oh, no, Lily." Saundra pulled a pair of overalls out of the closet. "Not bad dreams. Good dreams. Really good dreams. I only wish . . ." She stopped and looked back into the closet as if it were filled with the words she wanted to say.

"What?"

"I only wish they would come true." Her voice was sad again. Her strange, happy mood had disappeared.

"Then you'd really have something to feel guilty about."

Saundra stepped into her overalls and walked toward Lily. "That's my real problem."

"What?"

"I have nothing to feel guilty about."

"I'm sure you'll find something," said Lily.

"Promise?" asked Saundra, bringing her face close.

"Knowing you . . ." Lily began.

Saundra straightened up. "No one knows me. No one. Not even me."

"I know you," said Lily, hoping Saundra would believe her even if she wasn't so sure herself.

"I'm a deep, dark secret." And with that, Saundra grabbed her boots and walked from the room.

"Wait a minute!" Lily yelled after her.

But Saundra kept right on walking.

"You can't go to rehearsal like that. You don't have anything on under your overalls!"

Saundra was gone. And Lily shuddered to think her sister was trying to make her dream come true, in real life.

3

Hints

That same Saturday, soon after Saundra had left practically naked for rehearsal and the rest of the family was having lunch at home, Lily asked her parents, "What's the matter with Saundra these days?"

Her parents looked up from their food at the same time, put down their forks at the same time, looked at one another, and then turned their heads to look at her, both at the same time. Lily expected them to *speak* at the same time. But they didn't.

"A good question," said her father.

"We were wondering the same thing," said her mother.

Then they looked at one another again.

Lily looked at them looking at each other. She wondered what they were trying to communicate. Parents were great at giving one another puzzled looks and then suddenly nodding in agreement, when no one else in the world even knew what they were discussing with their looks, let alone what agreement they had reached. Parents were a mystery. They were such a mystery that she didn't understand how they understood each other half the time. But they did. Except this time all they understood was that they didn't understand what was going on with Saundra.

And in this family, when no one understood something, when there was a real mystery, it was usually left up to Lily to solve it. This was especially true when the mystery had to do with Saundra.

Saundra was now fifteen, and Lily knew from hearing things her parents had said that when someone was fifteen she suddenly seemed to close up like a clam, and she didn't say anything to anyone about anything, or at least about anything that might be bothering her. This didn't make Lily look forward to becoming fifteen, because she really liked to talk, even about her problems. But she still had five years until then, and she hoped that in five years' time maybe it would be different to be fifteen, maybe whatever laws of nature governed fifteenness would be altered and girls who were fifteen would find themselves not closed like a clam but open like a flower. She hoped, but she didn't count on it.

She also knew that a girl who was fifteen was much more likely to talk to her sister than to her parents. Lily's parents knew this too. That's why they left the solving of this particular mystery up to Lily.

"It would be good if you could talk to her," her mother said.

"But what am I going to say?"

"Ask her what's the matter," said her mother.

"I already did."

"Oh, good," said her father. "You're already on the case." He took a bite of his corned beef sandwich and ended up with a blond mustard-mustache. "And what did she say?"

"To make a long story short," said Lily, "she told me about her dreams."

"Aha!" said her mother, reaching over with her napkin to wipe off her husband's new mustache. "Dreams often reveal the unconscious truth."

"Boy, I hope not," said Lily. "You should hear about her dreams."

Her parents stopped eating and looked at her.

Lily had second thoughts. "You don't want to hear about her dreams."

"Oh, yes we do," they said.

"Dreams are the most private things there are," said Lily.

"Sometimes," said her father, who was a lawyer, "the rights of privacy must be sacrificed to the common good."

"What is that supposed to mean?" Lily asked.

"What that is supposed to mean," said her mother, who was not only a lawyer but a judge as well, "is that the family comes first. Privacy is one thing. Unhappiness is another. And Saundra is unhappy. So tell us."

"Tell you what?"

"Tell us about Saundra's dreams," said her mother.

Lily drank her whole glass of milk in one gulp, pretending it was beer so maybe she would get instantly drunk and pass out and not have to say anything. But all she felt was a long ripple of coldness running down her chest and into her stomach. It made her even more wide awake.

Running the words together, she said, "She dreams she's naked in front of some guy whose mind is a camera."

"His mind is a what?" said her father, who started to eat again so quickly that the meat fell out of the bread.

"A camera," Lily said.

"Why a camera?" her mother asked. "Did she tell you that? Maybe she's worried about a photo session for the ballet. Maybe *People* magazine is featuring young ballerinas and—"

"So her naked body will be printed indelibly on the film of his consciousness," Lily interrupted.

Now her father dropped his bread too.

"Saundra's been reading too much," her mother said calmly.

Now it was Lily's turn to be surprised. "Reading! Saundra doesn't read. You know that. Saundra thinks books are things that people put on their stomachs at night to help them fall asleep."

Her mother chuckled. "Like you," she said to her husband.

"If I've told you once, I've told you a hundred times—I have the world's only literate bellybutton. Even when my eyes are closed, it can read entire books."

"Yeah," said Lily. "And you should see it turn the pages."

Her father laughed, and she did too.

"In case anyone's forgotten," said her mother, "we were discussing Saundra."

"I prefer to forget," said her father. He looked at Lily. "What's this business about Saundra being imprinted on someone's camera?"

"Someone's consciousness," said Lily, thinking that even she sounded like a dodo when she said it. "And not Saundra. Saundra's naked body."

"I told you," said her father. "I prefer to forget." He started to put his sandwich back together.

"Well, we can't forget it. And we can't ignore it," said her mother. "Something is bothering Saundra, something much more profound than I had imagined. Something about her body. Something about being a woman perhaps. Something. And we have to find out what it is. I mean, she has been acting very strangely lately. This business about the dreams is only one thing. And that's just what she *says*. What about what she *does*? Have you seen her lately?" she asked her husband.

"Of course I've seen her. We all live here together, remember?"

"I mean, have you watched her? Have you listened to her? One day last week I found her staring at herself in the bathroom mirror."

"What's so strange about that?" asked Lily's father. "I'll bet she does that all the time. Look at that dancing school of hers—they have mirrors on all the walls. Dancers have to look in mirrors."

"What was strange about it was that the bathroom door was open. Saundra *never* keeps the bathroom door open, not even when she's only brushing her teeth or grabbing a tissue."

"She must have wanted you to see her," Lily said.

"I think so too," said her mother. "But when I stopped to watch her and started to talk to her, she ignored me for the longest time. And then, just once, she took her eyes from the mirror and looked at me and asked, 'Do you think I'm sexy?' "

"That's the name of a song," Lily informed them.

"Oh, I hope not," said her father, moving his hands toward his ears as if he thought someone was about to sing it to him.

"Regardless," said her mother, "I must admit I was a bit taken aback by her question. But I knew she was going through something and needed encouragement, so I told her, 'Yes, Saundra, I think you're sexy.' "

"What a strange thing for a mother to say," said her husband.

Lily had the urge to ask her mother if she thought she was sexy too, but instead she said, "So what did Saundra say when you told her she was sexy?"

"She said she was weird. That's all. Just weird."

"Boy, that is pretty weird," said Lily.

"Come to think of it," said her father, "the other day when I came home from work I found Saundra lying completely motionless on the living room floor with her eyes closed and her arms crossed over her chest."

"Like a princess in a coffin," said Lily.

Her father went on. "So I went over to Saundra and I said, 'How come you aren't at rehearsal?' And she whispered, 'I *am* at rehearsal.' And I said, 'This is from *Giselle*?' And she said, 'This is from *Saundra*. It's a new ballet.' And I made the mistake of saying, 'It doesn't look very exciting.' And she said, 'It isn't. It's my life. All I do is lie here waiting.' 'Waiting for what?' I asked. 'Waiting for yesterday,' she said. 'What happened yesterday?' I said. 'Nothing,' she answered. 'Then why not wait for tomorrow?' I asked. 'Because yesterday's nothing is better than tomorrow's nothing,' she said—'at least it's over.' Then she stopped talking. I tried to make her laugh by telling her that it looked like a ballet that was so simple that even I could perform in it and did she want me to lie down next to her and we could do a *pas de deux*. But she ignored me. She seemed to go into a trance. Nothing moved." He hesitated and looked sadly at Lily and her mother. "Nothing moved . . . except a tear that went down her cheek."

Lily's mother shook her head. "I wish you had told me."

"What good would it have done? She just isn't letting us in on her life these days. Our daughter is suffering, and she won't tell us why."

Lily thought again of fifteen-year-olds as clams, closed tight, yielding nothing. "Well, she's certainly giving us hints," she said. "Hints and more hints." Her parents nodded as she took a drink of milk. "Anyway," she went on, "Saundra doesn't know that much herself."

"Certainly she knows what's bothering her," said her mother.

"But maybe she's not admitting to herself what

it really is. Maybe she really does think she looks weird. I mean, Saundra is *gorgeous,* and everybody knows Saundra is gorgeous. Even I'm willing to admit it. And maybe Saundra thinks she's gorgeous, too, but she's trying to tell herself she looks weird because it's easier for her to feel bad over looking weird than over whatever it is that's really bothering her."

"In other words . . ." her father began before he started to scratch his head in befuddlement.

"In other words," said Lily, "nobody knows what the heck is going on. Especially not Saundra. Do you know what she told me? She told me that she's a deep, dark secret. That's what she said. A deep, dark secret."

"Hmmm," said her father.

"She's a mystery even to herself," said her mother.

"And you want me to solve it, right?" said Lily.

They looked at her, proudly and expectantly. And she felt great, in the moment before she got worried. How was she going to learn the secret of someone who was a deep, dark secret even to herself?

4

Suspicions

Ever since Lily had helped Saundra win her place in the second company of the American Ballet Center, her parents had made Lily a kind of honorary parent when it came to Saundra. It was almost as if they were relieved to let the two sisters work out their own problems and, when they did, become so close that they were best friends as well as sisters. Of course, their parents were always there to help if there was a problem that Lily and Saundra couldn't solve. But there almost never was. And Lily got the feeling that her parents actually enjoyed standing on the sidelines and not taking sides but just watching. Maybe it was a relief for them because of their jobs.

They were both lawyers. And one of them was a judge. People who didn't know them but knew that one of them was a judge seemed to assume that Mr. Leonard was the judge. But it was Mrs. Leonard who was the judge. And because she was a judge, no one who knew her and knew she was a judge called her Mrs. Leonard. She was Judge Leonard. Mr. Leonard loved it when they were introduced, properly, as Judge and Mr. Leonard. People who didn't know them were always surprised to hear them introduced that way. You could see such people looking quizzically at whoever had made the introduction, as if this person had lost his or her marbles or had gotten confused in the middle of a tongue twister. But that's what they were: Judge and Mr. Leonard.

But at home, they did not like to take sides or pass judgment.

Now, as Lily told them again that she would talk to Saundra, her father said with relief, "Thank goodness. She'll listen to you."

"Maybe she'll listen to me," Lily said. "But will she talk to me?"

"A valid distinction," her father said.

Lily wondered if he knew that the last time he'd used that expression she hadn't known what it meant, so she'd looked up the words in the dictionary. Now she knew what it meant. She also knew he was right.

"Very valid," she said.

"A veritable veracity," he responded, his eyes twinkling.

"Huh?" said Lily, before she could catch herself. She had fallen into his trap and had failed to pretend, as she always liked to do, that she

19

understood everything he said, especially when he was teasing her.

"Really, Harold," her mother said to her father, covering up for Lily. And to Lily she said, "He meant you're telling the truth."

"I always tell the truth," Lily said.

"To a fault," her mother said.

Now it was her father's turn to give her mother a taste of her own medicine. "Really, Florence," he said to her. Then he added, "What do you mean by that? How can it be a fault always to tell the truth?"

"There are some truths that should be kept to oneself," her mother answered.

"How can you say that?" her father asked her mother. "You're a judge, after all. 'The whole truth and nothing but the truth.' Isn't that what people are supposed to speak when they appear before you? Isn't that the oath they take?"

And to that Judge Leonard responded as she had many times before. "My home is not a courtroom. And my courtroom is certainly not a home. The problems that come up in court are much easier to solve than the problems that come up in a family. And the truths that are spoken in court, which are matters of fact, are much simpler than the truths that might be spoken at home, because the truths at home are not just facts, they are also opinions, and they are feelings, and they are sometimes not truths at all but impressions or even suspicions."

"Suspicions?" said Lily's father, bringing his hands up toward his face, as if he had something more to hide than the big smile he was smiling.

"Gee, Mom, are you suspicious of someone?" Lily asked, serious but also, like her father, teasing the Judge just a little bit.

Fortunately, Judge Leonard had a sense of humor also. "I'm suspicious of everybody," she said. "Everybody. No one escapes my suspicion. I suspect everybody . . . of making fun of me."

"It ain't hard," said Lily's father.

"What?" asked her mother. "Being suspicious of everybody?"

"No," said her father. "Making fun of you."

Her mother laughed. "Oh, I know. I sound terribly pompous sometimes. Especially when I'm serious about something. And I *am* serious about my home. My home is not a courtroom. One cannot be a judge of everything everywhere, and in one's home—"

"There she goes again," Lily's father interrupted.

Lily's mother looked surprised. Then her eyes glazed over as if she were turning them around and looking inside herself. And then her eyes cleared up completely as they squinted into a smile. "There I went again," she said. "Off the deep end, smack into the pool of pomposity."

Lily's father jumped out of his seat. "Well, let me dry you, then," he said, and he went to his wife and pretended to have a towel and rubbed her all over until she screamed that he was tickling her and he stopped.

She stood up and they hugged one another.

Lily, still in her seat, watched them and finally said, because she could think of nothing else to say, "Lovebirds."

"Cockadoodledoo," her father said.

"Really, Harold," her mother said to her father. "That's not a bird. That's a chicken."

"First of all," he replied, "a chicken is a bird. And secondly, that's not a chicken, that's a rooster."

"That's what I was afraid of," Lily's mother said, not looking afraid at all; looking pleased, as a matter of fact.

"What?" her father asked.

"That you're a rooster."

"Cockadoodledoo," he said again, leaving no doubt.

They couldn't fool Lily. She knew what was going on. It was always like this on Saturday, once they were done with lunch and Lily was about to leave for her ballet class and her parents were about to have the apartment all to themselves. They couldn't fool her when they started to play with one another like this. She had her suspicions. The moment she was out the door, they were going to start playing with one another once again. And one thing would lead to another. She didn't know where it was all going to end up. But one thing would certainly lead to another. And somewhere along the line—she wasn't sure where, but somewhere—there was going to be sex. That much she knew. They couldn't fool her. She wasn't even sure they wanted to.

"What time is your class?" her father asked.

As if he didn't know. "Three," she said.

"And you'll be coming home with Saundra?" her mother asked. "About six, right?" As if *she* didn't know.

Lily nodded. Then she thought for a moment, decided she might as well give it a try, and said, "That should give you guys enough time."

Both of them turned red at the same time. Both of them also tried to speak at the same time, but nothing came out of their mouths.

Rendered speechless, Lily thought, enjoying in her mind a phrase that she'd just read in a book and had memorized and had been waiting for the right opportunity to use to see if she knew what it really meant. Now she knew exactly. "Rendered speechless," she said aloud.

Her parents grew even redder. But now they burst out laughing together and reached out together to touch Lily on the head.

"Smart-ass," her father said with great affection.

"Too much for her own good," said her mother. "There are some truths that should be kept to oneself. There are some truths that are not truths at all, as I was saying before, but are impressions, suspicions—"

"There she goes again," said Lily, to save her mother embarrassment and also to show her father that she never missed a word he said.

"And there *you* go," he said, pointing toward the door.

Lily could take a hint. She hurried to her room, put a clean leotard and clean tights into her new canvas bag with her intitials on it, and headed for the front door.

But she couldn't resist what she thought they referred to in books by the phrase "a parting blow."

"Have fun, you guys," she said to her parents and learned once again, from the way they shook their heads, that she knew exactly what that phrase meant, too.

5

Money
and
Misery

Lily took the bus down Central Park West, got off at Sixty-sixth Street, and walked the one block west to Broadway and the American Ballet Center. She could have waited for the bus itself to cut over to Broadway, but she had made it a custom to walk down Sixty-sixth Street, since that was the street that Saundra had led her down last year, when Lily was going to her very first class at ABC and was so scared about it that she'd lain down on the sidewalk of this very same street and had pretended to have a case of numb legs.

What a lame excuse that had been, Lily thought now and smiled at what she figured was a pretty good pun. And how lucky for her that Saundra hadn't believed it for a moment. Otherwise Lily might never have gone to dancing school that day, and then she would have missed out on one of the great pleasures of life. It wasn't so much that she wanted to be a dancer or was even very good at it. She just loved to dance. She loved her class, learning to master the technique that Miss Witt, her wonderfully awful teacher, said was the most important thing of all. Lily still remembered Miss Witt's speech from the first class: "Without technique, none of you will ever be a dancer. Dance is first of all technique. Technique, technique, technique! There is nothing you can do in dance without technique. There is no step, no leap, no arabesque, no *écart*, otherwise known as a split, no *cabriole*, no *ballon*, no anything—there is nothing that can be mastered without technique. Am I understood?"

Was she understood? It was just like Miss Witt to ask a question like that. Was she understood? Miss Witt said things so directly, and in such a loud, high voice, and she repeated herself so many times, that it was impossible *not* to understand her. Understanding Miss Witt wasn't the problem. But doing what she wanted often was. Dance was terribly difficult. It was one thing to understand what you were supposed to do. It was another thing entirely to do it.

Still, Lily loved it. She loved the class and she loved the technique and she loved the very exercise of it—the bending and stretching, the sweating and groaning, and, yes, even the pain— and she also loved practicing at home, which consisted of just kind of staying in shape, doing a lot of stretching exercises and using her mind to accomplish what Miss Witt called "absorbing technique, becoming technique," which was a major step on the way to becoming not only a dancer but dance itself.

Not that Lily planned to become a dancer. Saundra was the dancer in the family, a real one, who learned roles and danced in public before people who had paid money in order to watch her and who herself was paid money, though Saundra had explained to Lily that it was just a little bit of money and that no matter how good she became as a dancer, or even how famous, she would still be paid just a little bit of money, at least compared to what other people were paid, and not just people like lawyers and judges but also people like truck drivers and cooks. Saundra had even shown her an article about Saundra's idol, Suzanne Farrell, who danced with the New York City Ballet and who said, "You'll never make a lot of money in ballet. It's something we do because we love it, and we have to do it to be happy. Most dancers wouldn't know what to do with a lot of money anyway, because they wouldn't have time to spend it."

That was for sure. One of the reasons Lily had decided not to try to become a real dancer, aside from the fact that she knew in her very bones that she was not good enough to become a real dancer, that she was not a born dancer, was the time that it would take. She was perfectly happy going to class once a week and doing a bit of stretching and strengthening on the other six days. But she didn't want to be like Saundra. She didn't want to go to class every day and rehearsals every day and still have to practice at home and watch her diet constantly and thus feel that every time she ate an ice-cream cone she was committing

27

a sin against her body. She wasn't sure what she did want to do. She wasn't even sure whether she had been born to do something in particular, the way Saundra seemed to have been born to be a dancer.

Saundra gave her life to the dance. So dance was her life. This meant that whatever was bothering her, it must have something to do with dancing.

So Lily, walking to the American Ballet Center, knew she was going to the right place. This was where Saundra really lived her life.

This was where Lily would discover the key to the mystery of Saundra's misery.

To discover anything in ABC was like looking for a needle in a haystack, an expression that had always filled Lily not with a sense of how difficult that might be but with a dread of haystacks: she imagined sticking her hand into the haystack and having no trouble at all finding the needle—it would be right there, stuck into her hand!

Sometimes she felt the same way about the American Ballet Center. It was not so much that it was difficult to find things there as that it was painful. There were so many girls (and there were beginning to be quite a few boys, too), and the competition was so intense among those who wanted to be serious dancers that you had to be careful whom you talked to and whom you praised and even whom you were seen walking next to in the long, dark, drafty corridors.

The fact that she was the sister of Saundra Leonard, who was one of the young stars of the school, was both good and bad for Lily. It made a lot of people act nicely to Lily, because they wanted Saundra to act nicely to them. And it made a lot of people act rotten to Lily, because they envied Saundra, which made them think they hated her too, and tried to take it out on Lily.

It never got as bad as it had been at the beginning, when even Saundra had turned against her because Saundra had thought Lily was in cahoots with Meredith Meredith and hadn't yet realized that Lily was the only one capable of intimidating Meredith Meredith sufficiently to allow Saundra to win the audition. That was a terrible time, before she and Saundra had become friends.

But there was still trouble with Meredith Meredith. She had never forgiven Saundra for beating her out for the place in the second company. And while she was too dumb to realize just how Lily had intimidated her into losing and had encouraged Saundra into winning, Meredith Meredith hated Lily just for being Saundra's sister. This didn't mean that she said nasty things to Lily. In fact, she gave both Lily and Saundra the silen' treatment. Meredith Meredith took every opportunity either to ignore Lily and Saundra or to snub them by turning away when either of them came near her or to scorn them by giving them burning looks with her ice-blue eyes and snarling at them with her enormous lips and raising her bony shoulders when they approached, the way an angry cat raises its back.

None of this had changed when Meredith Meredith herself had won a place of her own in the second company, about six months after Saundra had won hers. Meredith Meredith was a wonderful dancer, there was no doubting that. Saundra had always admitted, if only to Lily, that she thought Meredith Meredith might be an even better dancer than she was herself. And Meredith Meredith was beautiful, too, with her golden hair and blue eyes and terrific skinny figure, though Lily could only see her beauty like something apart from Meredith Meredith; she couldn't feel it because she knew Meredith Meredith was unkind and jealous and vindictive and thus was falsely beautiful. Only her body was beautiful. She was an ugly person.

Lily knew this from experience, and it was why she had so much trouble even seeing the beauty that Meredith Meredith carried around as if it had been glued onto her body.

Even the way Meredith Meredith had won her place in the company. . . . One of the girls already in the company—a very nice girl who was nearly eighteen and had been generous in making Saundra feel at home and as little frightened as possible when she was brand new and, after that, when she was learning new roles—had injured herself. She had failed to tell anyone that her Achilles tendons were becoming sore and swollen, because she didn't want to be told that she must give up her hard-won roles and take a rest (and for a dancer to rest, Lily knew, was like for a bird to stop flying—it happened only when she was starved or weary or momentarily curious about what the world was like at a standstill). And so one of her tendons had snapped. And that was that. They put her to bed. And, Saundra said, though Lily knew she was exaggerating, they forgot about her.

To take her place in the company, though not

immediately to fill her actual roles, they chose Meredith Meredith. Meredith Meredith had come in second to Saundra the last time there was an audition. It had seemed only right that she now join the company. Even Saundra agreed with this, though she didn't really like the idea of dancing with Meredith Meredith. "She might set my costumes on fire with her dirty looks," Saundra told Lily, exaggerating again.

So Meredith Meredith got her place in the second company. But rather than finally making up with her arch rival, Meredith Meredith became even more snarly and cold toward Saundra, as if she were determined to share nothing with her, even though Meredith Meredith now had what she had always wanted: a place in the company.

So Lily decided that whatever was the matter with Saundra, it involved the American Ballet Center and the only other princess in the place, Meredith Meredith.

And it wasn't long until she found out that she was right.

6

Here Comes Meredith Meredith

Lily undressed for class in the same large and ugly room in which she'd first, so timidly a year ago, gone into contortions in order to get out of her street clothes and into her dance clothes without anyone seeing her in her underpants.

She couldn't believe she'd been so shy. Now she thought nothing of getting completely undressed—she'd learned you had to bring a clean pair of underpants to replace the ones you'd sweated up during class—and standing right there, naked, by the bench. Sometimes she even walked across the room with nothing on, in order to say something to Saundra or to try to find one of her sneakers. She didn't do this to show off. Hardly. But neither was Lily ashamed of her body. She used to think it was a bit chubby. And maybe it had been. But her dancing had made her body harder on the outside and, more important, somehow tougher when she felt it from the inside. And while she couldn't explain just how you went about feeling your body from the inside, she knew you could, because she did it all the time. And most of the time—if she'd gotten enough exercise and hadn't recently attacked a pizza like a lawnmower gone berserk—it felt just terrific.

As Lily put on her leotard and tights and slippers, she looked around and realized that the room was filled with people, as it always was—classes and rehearsals began and ended at different times in all the different rooms, so kids were constantly spilling in and out of what was supposed to be the girls' dressing room, though sometimes boys used it too, the way girls sometimes used the boys' dressing room. There were always people around, changing their clothes, resting, drying off their sweaty bodies, drinking diet soda, "borrowing" pieces of gum from one another, putting on makeup, putting their hair into dance buns, and talking, always talking, exchanging the latest gossip about who was dancing well and who was making a fool of herself and who had gained weight and who had lost enough weight to be too weak to dance and who had managed to find a boyfriend.

But for all the talk that went on all the time, Lily didn't join in on it very often. For one thing, she attended the school only once a week, on Saturdays, so she didn't know the other people all that well. And for another, she had her sister to talk to and go home with after class. She didn't need new friends all that much when her very best friend in the world was right there with her.

But today, someone came along to talk to her.

Someone actually came looking for her as she was getting ready to go to class. And who should it be but the only enemy that she and Saundra had in the world: Meredith Meredith!

She and Meredith Meredith hadn't spoken to one another since Lily had intimidated her right into losing the audition. It had been nearly a year ago. Since then, not a word from Meredith Meredith. Only the silent treatment, the snub.

Until this moment. Meredith Meredith was right there next to her. And it was no accident that she was standing there, her eyes blazing, her giant lips in a sneer even as she spoke.

"Tell your sister she doesn't have a chance."

It was exactly the same thing Meredith Meredith had said to her last year, just before she had hurt Lily by pinching her hips and Lily had slapped her face in return. But at least then it had made sense: Saundra and Meredith Meredith had been in competition for the one place in the company. But now both of them were in the company. It didn't make any sense at all. Lily thought Meredith Meredith must have forgotten that the competition was over.

"She doesn't need a chance," Lily said, standing up from the bench in the hope that it would make some difference, though it was most discouraging to find that the top of her head was even with Meredith Meredith's chest, where her tiny breasts, so perfect for ballet, were flattened by her leotard.

"She doesn't *have* a chance," Meredith Meredith repeated.

Lily decided that the best way to get rid of

Meredith Meredith was to play her own game. "She doesn't *need* a chance," she said.

"Stop repeating yourself," said Meredith Meredith.

Oh, boy, thought Lily, what a dope. Aloud, she said, "Why should she need a chance at something if she already has everything she wants?"

"Because she doesn't," said Meredith Meredith, bending over so those lips of hers almost touched Lily's ear.

"I *know* she doesn't," Lily said. "That's what I just told you."

Meredith Meredith straightened and sucked her lips back into her mouth. At the same time her eyes rolled up nearly all the way into her forehead. She looked terrible and ridiculous at the same time. She stayed like that for a while, completely still. Then Lily realized that this must be Meredith Meredith's way of thinking.

Finally Meredith Meredith relaxed. Her lips popped out and her eyes settled down. And, after giving the whole matter one more thought, this time squinching up her whole face so that her eyes actually disappeared into her cheeks, she spoke, "You did?"

Yikes! After all that, all she could do was ask a dumb question that wasn't even a real question. Lily wasn't going to give her any help. So she merely answered, "Yup."

"You did?"

Lily couldn't take it anymore. She spoke fast. "That's right, I did. You said my sister doesn't have a chance. I said my sister doesn't need a chance. You said she doesn't. I said I know she

35

doesn't. And then you asked me if I said I know she doesn't. And I said yup, that I certainly do know that I said my sister doesn't need a chance. Is that clear?"

Once again Meredith Meredith ate her lips and lost her eyes in her forehead. And when she finally returned to normal, she said, "Wait a minute."

So Lily waited. She said nothing. Let Meredith Meredith get out of this one by herself.

"Wait a minute," she repeated.

Apparently she wanted another minute to squinch up her face again and give the whole thing a bit more thought. Lily waited.

All of a sudden Meredith Meredith's face flew open, her eyes shining, her white teeth bared, sweat jumping off her skin. "Didn't you say your sister had everything she wants?"

Lily nodded.

"Well, she doesn't!" said Meredith Meredith triumphantly. "And she doesn't have a chance to get it!"

At that moment Lily realized that she might have found the needle in the haystack, the key to the mystery of Saundra's misery. If there was something Saundra wanted, and she didn't have it, then maybe not having it was what was making her so sad these days and so difficult to get along with. And Meredith Meredith knew what it was.

Should Lily ask her what it was? Even as she wondered whether that was the smart thing to do, Meredith Meredith turned on her heel, stuck her nose in the air, and walked away looking like a whooping crane that's had ballet lessons. But at the door to the dressing room, she turned around again and shouted back at Lily, "Tell her she doesn't have a *chance!*"

7

The Confession

After her class, and after Saundra's rehearsal, they met as usual in the dressing room. Lately, because Saundra was often in a miserable mood or spoke such nonsense when she wasn't, Lily had done most of the talking. She would try to cheer Saundra up even before Saundra spoke, because Lily could tell from the way Saundra let her body and her mouth droop that she was sad and frustrated and in no mood to say anything, or at least anything nice or anything sensible. So Lily always spoke first and filled the air with conversation just so she wouldn't have to listen to Saundra complain or be nasty or tell her some crazy fantasy.

But today Lily decided to be silent. She was tempted to speak right away just to say something to Saundra, who was saying absolutely nothing but was merely sulking at the same time as she stripped out of her dance clothes and put on—instead of her usual fancy tight jeans and silk blouse and the high boots she wore no matter what the season— those ridiculous overalls with nothing under them except Saundra's beautiful body, which you could catch a glimpse of whenever Saundra moved or even breathed.

And Lily almost broke her vow of silence when finally Saundra spoke.

Except it wasn't exactly speech. Saundra didn't really say anything. She just went, "Ohhhh." It was a sigh, a moan.

Lily's impulse was to say, "What's the matter?" But she put her teeth together and said nothing. Saundra had never moaned quite like that before. It sounded as if it had come from the very center of her, and without her wanting it to. It made Lily feel sad and excited at the same time.

"Oh, shit," said Saundra.

Wow! That was better than a moan, even if it was a bit unpleasant. Lily's impulse now was to say, "Watch your tongue," but instead she held her own.

"What am I going to do?" asked Saundra mournfully.

And Lily knew that now the conversation had finally begun.

"About what?" she asked.

"Ohhhh," said Saundra, drawing out the word but not quite moaning it this time.

"Ohhhh what?" asked Lily.

"Oh . . . I don't know."

Lily knew that Saundra did know. She also knew that Saundra wanted to tell her. But Lily wasn't sure she wanted to hear what Saundra had to say. What if Saundra told her something truly horrible? What if Lily were powerless to do anything about it? What if Saundra . . .

"I'm in love."

"What!"

But that was it. Saundra had told her everything in three little words. Or was it four, if you counted the contraction? Yikes, why was she thinking about that? Three little words. Four little words. Saundra had told her everything. Or at least everything she was going to tell her. For she didn't say another word.

By the time Lily had recovered from her shock over Saundra's confession, Saundra had thrown her dance bag over her shoulder and was headed toward the door of the dressing room, her overalls moving back and forth off her skin with each step she took.

"Wait."

But Saundra was gone.

Lily thought of chasing after her, but as she thought this she also sank down onto the bench.

She sat, chin in her hand, elbows on her knees, eyes looking down at her Adidases, which rested on the floor one on top of the other like a puppy's paws. This was her thinking position. But she didn't know what to think. She didn't even know where to start thinking. And she wouldn't have been able to hear her own thoughts anyway. All she could hear in her mind were Saundra's words: "I'm in love."

In love! What did that mean?

Well, Lily knew what it was supposed to mean,

she'd read it in books and heard it in movies often enough. But what did it mean for Saundra? If Saundra was in love, what did it have to do with what she was going through these days? Surely you didn't jump for joy one minute and crumble the next and dream disturbing dreams and consider yourself a deep, dark secret and act crabby and distant and cold just because you were in love. Did you?

Love was supposed to be nice, wasn't it? Maybe *being* in love wasn't. Yet how could that be? How could Lily help her sister if she didn't even understand what was happening to her sister?

Thoughts poured through her mind. Questions that she could not answer. Hold your tongue, she told herself, but she could not control that voice. She longed for silence within herself.

8
The Autograph

"Did you tell her she doesn't have a chance?"

Lily looked up. Meredith Meredith stood over her, looking more gorgeous than ever in an unusual way. A sheen of sweat covered every inch of her skin and made Lily think of the world's most perfect glazed doughnut.

Meredith Meredith had a white towel draped around her neck, its ends hanging over her small breasts. Her leotard was stained. And the sweat at the top of her forehead had turned her blond hair dark.

One thing about Meredith Meredith: she might be mean and nasty, but she worked just as hard as anyone else at her dancing. Her sweat dripped down on Lily. It was like a visit from a great athlete. A star.

"Can I have your autograph?" Lily asked.

Meredith Meredith looked surprised. "How come?"

"To preserve forever," said Lily. "You're famous."

"I know I am." Meredith Meredith actually went on point when she said that and did several complete turns, brushing Lily with her sweat and her perfume. But by the time she stopped and came down, there was a look of suspicion on her face. "Famous as what?"

"As yourself," said Lily. "Of course."

Meredith Meredith scratched the trail made by a drop of sweat down her neck. "Oh, yeah, right."

"And as a dancer," Lily added.

Meredith Meredith almost went up on point again. "Naturally," she said.

"And as a famous beauty."

She thought Meredith Meredith was going to kiss her, so close did she lean, so wildly did her eyelids flutter.

"And as a brain." Lily wondered how far she could go before Meredith Meredith started to fly around the room on the wings of flattery.

But she was smarter than Lily had thought. For the second time, she looked at Lily suspiciously. "As a what?"

"A brain."

"Hey, did you hear that one?" Meredith Meredith called out to a bunch of girls lounging on benches across the room. "Saundra's sister is so dumb she thinks I'm smart."

All the girls laughed, all but one. She took a drag on her cigarette, with a pained expression on her face, and then said in a smoke-chained voice, "No one's that dumb."

All the girls laughed again, until they saw Meredith Meredith glaring at them. "What's that supposed to mean, Aurora?" she said to the girl.

"You're a great dancer, Double M," Aurora said, "but in the brains department you've got a permanent vacancy sign hanging off your nose."

"At least I can dance," said Meredith Meredith.

Aurora flicked her cigarette at Meredith Meredith. It hit her white towel. Sparks flew off.

"What aim!" said Aurora proudly. "I should be a sharpshooter. I don't know why I spend my time dancing."

"I don't either." Meredith Meredith examined her towel. When she found an ash, she blew it off. "You're a terrible dancer."

"Just not terrible enough." Aurora lit another cigarette. "If I were as bad a dancer as you are dumb, maybe they'd let me quit."

"*She* doesn't think I'm dumb." Meredith Meredith pointed at Lily, who was beginning to think she should never have started to tease Meredith Meredith. "She even wants my autograph."

"Wow!" said a couple of the girls, who took such things seriously.

"Your autograph!" said Aurora.

"And I'm going to give it to her," said Meredith Meredith. "You got a piece of paper?" she asked Lily.

Lily shook her head. This had gone too far.

"Gimme a piece of paper," Meredith Meredith shouted toward the girls on the benches. A few of them started to scurry around. "And a pencil." Now they scurried faster. In dancing schools, there are always handmaidens to serve the princess.

Finally one of the girls found a clean white sheet with the American Ballet Center letterhead, and another one handed Meredith Meredith her felt-tipped pen with a tiny statue of John Travolta at the top of it that had loose shoes so he danced when you wrote something.

Meredith Meredith put the paper down on the bench and held the pen poised over it as if she were about to sign the Declaration of Independence.

"What do you want me to say?"

"Just make an X," said Aurora from across the room. Some of the girls laughed again.

"I know how to write," said Meredith Meredith haughtily. "Quick," she said to Lily in a whisper, "what do you want me to say?"

And Lily understood that Meredith Meredith really couldn't think of anything to say and wanted her to help.

"Well, how do you really feel about me?" Lily asked.

"I hate your guts."

"Okay," said Lily.

"Okay what?"

"Say that."

"In my autograph?"

"Sure."

"Hey, great!" Meredith Meredith smiled gleefully and put the pen in her mouth as she stared down at the paper, aiming or maybe trying to picture how the words would look.

"Hey, you're eating John Travolta!" said the girl who had given her the pen.

Meredith Meredith gave the girl a dirty look but removed John Travolta's head from between her large, wet lips and wrote:

I HATE YOUR GUTS
Meredith Meredith

Lily was surprised by her handwriting. She thought it would look like a little kid's printing. But it was real writing, with all kinds of loops and hoops and extra lines connecting the letters and tear-shaped dots over the *i*'s in her name. It was writing that danced.

"Here," she said, handing Lily the paper. "Anything for my fans." And with that, Meredith Meredith went up on point and started to walk across the room to her friends. Halfway there, she turned around and said to Lily, "On second thought, that autograph is for your sister. And don't forget to tell her she doesn't have a chance."

"A chance at what?" her friends asked.

Meredith Meredith started to move her hips as if she were on one of those waist-reducing machines that threw you around inside a giant rubber band.

The other girls whistled and laughed.

Lily shook her head without moving it. What was she going to do with a hate letter and a message to Saundra that seemed to say she didn't have a chance at gyrating her behind in front of a bunch of giggling teen-agers?

9

Saturday Night School

They always ate together on Saturday night. It was a family tradition. And it was often the only night of the week that all four of them were home for the evening meal. On week nights, Judge and Mr. Leonard, or at least one of them, usually had to work late at the office and so couldn't make it to dinner with the rest of them. Saundra's rehearsals went on through the dinner hour. If she were performing, she would be home at dinner time but liked to rest in her room rather than eat, and this she was permitted to do. Only Lily was always available. When you were ten years old, you could be counted on to be home for dinner. When you were ten years old, the world wasn't ready for you to wander around within it whenever you wanted. And your parents weren't willing.

But of course they knew it wouldn't be long. Her father in particular seemed both sad and happy that his girls were getting older and growing up. And he was the one who most insisted that they keep to the tradition of eating together on Saturday night.

"We'll always be a family," he would say, "but we won't always be together. Someday you kids will go off to college. But a long time before that you're going to go off to Saturday Night School."

"What's Saturday Night School?" Lily had asked the first time she'd heard the term.

Her father had laughed. "That's where you go to learn all the things that no one ever teaches you at home."

"Like what?" Lily had asked.

At the same time, Saundra had said, "Oh, Dad."

He had laughed some more and hadn't answered Lily's question.

By now she felt she understood. Saturday Night School was supposed to be the exciting part of life, where you did things that you couldn't do at home and wouldn't do at home and probably shouldn't do at home. Lily suspected that these things had something to do with boys and with sex. She would like to know for sure, but her curiosity was only to know, not to do. She didn't mind at all staying home on Saturday night for dinner. In fact, she loved this time when the whole family sat around together and caught up on their lives.

Tonight, because of Saundra's confession about being in love, Lily felt they had a lot of catching up to do. But she didn't know how to talk about it without Saundra's permission, and from the glum way Saundra sat at the table, Lily couldn't imagine Saundra granting permission even to give her a hug, let alone to give away her secret.

So Lily was grateful when her mother asked what she'd done in class today.

"*Fouettés.*"

"What's that?" her father asked.

"*Fouetté* means whipped," she replied. "In French."

"What does it mean in ballet?" he asked.

"Whipped," Lily answered.

"You mean you get whipped?" he joked. Before Lily could answer, he said to his wife, "Do you mean to tell me we're sending our children to a school where they get whipped?"

Their mother seemed to take his question seriously for a moment, looking perplexed and worried, but then she smiled mischievously and said, "A little discipline never hurt anyone."

"A little discipline!" said Lily, pretending to believe that her mother believed that they actually whipped the students at the American Ballet Center.

"A little *whipping*," said her father in a low, mean voice that made both Lily and her mother laugh at his silly villainy.

Her father got up from his chair and tried to look mean, like Fagin or Long John Silver, and hobbled around the table saying gruff words about whipped ballerinas, but pretty soon he started to laugh, too, and couldn't control his voice, so that all his evil words came out sounding as if they'd been spoken by chipmunks.

49

It was all most enjoyable until Saundra began to cry.

The last time Lily had heard Saundra cry was a year ago, when she wept in the middle of the night because dancing had made her feet ugly and she wasn't sure it was worth it if she couldn't be a great dancer and couldn't win the audition. Since then, and since winning the audition, if Saundra had cried—and until this moment Lily doubted she had—then she had cried in private.

But now here she was, crying right at the dinner table, crying at the same time that everyone else was laughing their heads off.

The laughter stopped abruptly. For a while there was no sound except for the sound of Saundra's crying and the strange, empty sound made by the shocked silence of Lily and her parents.

Finally their father spoke.

"What's the matter, princess?"

Saundra just shook her head and kept on crying. Lily watched her and felt terrible that she was so unhappy and at the same time tried to figure out what was going on. Something was different. And it wasn't just that Saundra was crying.

"Perhaps we were too raucous," said Judge Leonard apologetically.

Saundra shook her head at her mother to say that that wasn't it, and still she sat there and cried.

Now Lily understood! Saundra wasn't moving. She wasn't going anywhere. She wasn't leaving the table. In the past, Saundra would get up and go at the least provocation. She was always excusing herself—or sometimes, when she was really upset, not even excusing herself—when the least thing bothered her. She was always taking off for their room, where Lily would later find her either lying on her bed sulking or, more often, doing her dance exercises so strenuously that she was sweating and nearly out of breath and had a glazed look in her eyes.

Now Saundra had a terrific excuse to leave the table—her tears and whatever pain was causing them—but she didn't leave. She just sat there and wept. It was like when she had left the bathroom door open and their mother had found her telling herself she looked weird. Saundra was trying to tell them something. But Lily also knew that Saundra wasn't very good at telling things, at being normal and nice and saying things about herself. Even that afternoon, when she had said something so surprising and strange to Lily, she had then immediately disappeared out the door of the dressing room, just the way she always disappeared from the dinner table. But at least she had said *something* about herself. She had made a brief confession. And while Lily had felt at first that Saundra wouldn't like her telling other people about it, now she felt that Saundra wanted just that. Why else was she putting herself through the pain and embarrassment of remaining at the table in tears while everyone else looked at her and didn't know what to say and wanted only to help her if only they knew how?

Lily took a terrible chance and said, "I think I know what's the matter."

She was speaking to her parents when she

said this, but she didn't look at them, she looked at Saundra. She figured that Saundra knew what she was going to say, and if Saundra was going to object, this was her chance to do it, by giving Lily a dirty look or even by screaming at her to shut up. She did nothing but keep on crying. Lily was on her own.

"You do?" said her father.

"Tell us, Lily, please, if you don't mind," said her mother.

"Well," Lily began, "Saundra's—"

At that moment, Lily was interrupted by a terrible scream. Saundra's eyes were shut, her shoulders shook uncontrollably, and her mouth was wide open, shrieking a sound of great sadness.

Both their parents jumped up together and approached Saundra from either side, bending down when they reached her so their faces were next to hers. Saundra usually didn't like people to be close to her and touch her, but she did nothing to stop them. They clutched her and touched her face to wipe away her endless tears and looked into her face when they weren't looking at each other with a puzzled and concerned expression.

Lily could tell they were at a loss. In the midst of Saundra's painful outburst they'd forgotten that Lily had been about to tell them what she thought was the matter with Saundra. But now Lily couldn't believe that she'd had the answer. If Saundra really was in love, it couldn't be love that was making her so miserable. Surely, love couldn't do that to a person.

Lily decided she'd been wrong. Whatever was

bothering Saundra lately and making her cry now couldn't be love. It had to be something else. But what?

And then she remembered.

Meredith Meredith.

At dancing school, Lily had decided against telling Saundra what Meredith Meredith had said to her, figuring that Saundra herself would reveal the mystery of her misery. But all Saundra had said, before disappearing, was that she was in love. And love just couldn't be the cause of so much misery.

So it had to be Meredith Meredith. It had to be that needle in that haystack—it had to be whatever it was that Meredith Meredith said Saundra didn't have a chance to get.

But what?

It still didn't make sense. Their competition for a place in the company was over, especially now that both of them were in the company. It didn't make sense . . . until Lily thought of something else.

Her parents were still huddled on either side of Saundra, trying to comfort her. They had succeeded in that Saundra was no longer wailing, but her tears continued to fall silently.

Lily did not want to stop her parents from calming Saundra down, but suddenly she felt she had the answer to the whole thing.

"Saundra," she said, "Saundra. Are you and Meredith Meredith in competition for a part in a ballet?"

Saundra lifted her head, opened her eyes,

and looked at Lily. Her eyelids were swollen and strangely beautiful that way, shiny and large and terribly delicate-looking. But her eyes themselves were red from being filled with the salt of her tears. Lily's own eyes stung just to look at her sister's.

Saundra's voice was high and weak and raspy because she had been wailing. "Why?" she asked. "Why? What makes you . . . ?"

Lily waited for Saundra to complete the question, but Saundra could say no more. She seemed to be waiting for an answer.

"She came up to me while I was changing for class," Lily said. "She—"

"What did she say to you?" Suddenly Saundra was sitting up straight.

"She told me that you don't have a chance. But what I didn't understand—"

"She said *that*?"

Lily nodded.

"She said *that*!" Saundra repeated.

"Yes. But—"

"That I don't have a chance?"

"A chance at what?" their father said, and Lily was grateful for his words.

"A chance . . . a chance . . ." Saundra couldn't get the words out."

"At what?" their mother asked.

"At *living*," Saundra said. She rose slowly from her chair, turned, and walked away toward her room.

"Saundra . . ." their mother said mournfully, "please. . . . What do you mean? What could be so bad that—?"

But Saundra just kept going.

Her parents looked at Lily together. Their eyes were pleading with her. She knew what they wanted. She got up and followed Saundra. This time she wasn't going to let her get away.

10

A
Dead
Kielbasa

Saundra was curled up on her bed. It was unusual to see Saundra curled up, unless it was in the middle of some kind of dance exercise, and even then, most dance exercises stretched you out, they didn't curl you up. Saundra's usual position, whether she was awake or asleep, standing or sitting or lying down, was *straight*. Saundra was not the kind of person you would think of who would bend very much, who would be flexible except to dance, who would be anything but straight, straight and hard and difficult to move.

Lily had sometimes thought that if Saundra were to be made to bend, she might break. And Lily, looking at her now on the bed, realized that perhaps Saundra had broken. Even before the audition with Meredith Meredith she had not been this upset, this sad and troubled. It was as if something had snapped her in two and yet left her body in one piece.

Lily walked slowly toward her sister's bed. She wasn't even sure Saundra knew she was in the room.

"Saundra."

There was no reply.

"Saundra?"

Nothing.

For a second Lily thought of pouncing on her sister. That would certainly get her attention. But it was completely the wrong way to handle this situation.

She said Saundra's name one more time, and when Saundra still didn't answer, Lily decided that they weren't going to get anywhere if they didn't talk, and if that meant that only one of them was going to talk, then only one of them was going to talk. At least Saundra would listen. Even if she didn't want to, she would listen. What choice did she have, curled up on the bed just a few feet away?

"As I was saying to Mom and Dad before I was so rudely interrupted by your screaming like a maniac," Lily began, "you are in love. Right? Right. How do I know you're in love? Because you told me you're in love. Now, I may not know very much about being in love, since I'm only ten years old and I don't have breasts or anything and all the boys I know act like they're from the planet of the apes, but I do know this: being in love can't be so terrible a thing that it would make someone who *is* in love as miserable as you are right now. Right? Right. Okay. So if it's not being in love that's making you so miserable, then it must be something else. What? To tell you the truth, I don't know, but I'll bet it has something to do with Meredith Meredith. Right? Ri—"

"Yes."

Lily almost jumped, she was so surprised to hear Saundra say anything. For a moment, she was speechless. Then she waited to give Saundra a chance to say something more. But Saundra just lay there curled up, not moving, her head buried in her arms. Lily decided not to press her luck by waiting any longer.

"Well," she continued, "it has something to do with Meredith Meredith, just as I figured. And if it has to do with Meredith Meredith, then it must have something to do with dancing. Right? Right."

"Wrong."

"It doesn't have to do with Meredith Meredith?"

"I didn't say that." Saundra's voice was muffled because her mouth was buried beneath her arms and might even be filled with pillow, for all Lily knew. But at least it was her voice. At least she'd said more than one word without stopping.

"What *does* it have to do with then?"

Saundra said nothing in reply, but for the first time her body moved. She shook it, moving it as if she were shaking her head, saying no with her entire body.

Lily couldn't stand it any longer. "Saundra, I'm sick of this. If you want to talk to me, talk to me. If you don't want to talk to me, don't talk to me. But please stop lying there like a dead kielbasa."

Saundra started whimpering. And Lily thought, Oh, no, she's crying again. I never should have issued an ultimatum like that.

But right in the middle of Lily's thought, Saundra changed position for the first time. She turned over, still whimpering, and Lily saw what she had thought she might never see again: a smile on Saundra's face.

"What the hell is a dead kielbasa?"

"I thought you'd never ask," Lily said and, full of hope, knelt down beside her sister and reached out for her hands. Saundra let Lily put her fingers within her fingers, but she didn't clutch Lily the way Lily clutched her. Lily figured Saundra was weak from crying. And also that it was so much harder for Saundra to show her feelings than it was for Lily, or at least her good feelings.

"So?" Saundra asked.

"Okay. A dead kielbasa is—"

"Not that." Saundra smiled again. "I don't want to talk about that."

"What then?"

"You know."

"No, I don't," Lily said, though she did. She wanted Saundra to say it.

"I want to talk about me," said Saundra, looking away from Lily, who realized that her haughty and beautiful sister didn't really think she was all that great.

"What about you?" Lily asked, leading Saundra along. "What part of you do you want to talk about?"

"My heart."

"Is there something wrong with your heart?"

"It's broken."

It sounded so dramatic when Saundra said that, and yet Lily believed her and was shocked to hear someone actually say those words in real life. A broken heart. Was it possible? Did such things really happen?

She took her hand from Saundra's hand and brought it up and put it on Saundra's heart. She didn't know why she did that. It just happened. Perhaps she was curious to know if she could feel the brokenness. But she couldn't. She could feel only the hardness of the muscles in Saundra's chest and, beneath her little finger, the softness of her breast.

"You can't feel it, but it's there," said Saundra, seeming to read her thoughts.

"Does it hurt?"

Saundra nodded slowly. "And in my stomach."

"Do you have a broken stomach too?"

Saundra sat up abruptly. "It's not funny, Lily!"

Lily felt bad. She shouldn't have joked. "I'm sorry," she said. "But I just don't know about this kind of thing. If you have a broken heart, what broke it?"

"What do you think?"

"Love?"

Saundra nodded again, even more slowly.

"Love?" Lily asked again.

"Don't keep saying that word," Saundra said. "Just hearing it makes everything hurt even more."

"You make it sound as if love is torture."

"It is."

"Do you really mean that?"

"Love is terrible," Saundra said, and then she repeated it: "Love is terrible."

"May I tell you something?" Lily asked.

Saundra nodded.

"I don't believe you."

"Well, it's true," Saundra said emphatically.

"Maybe it is true, but I still don't believe you."

"Why?"

"Because I don't want to believe you. I love you, and it's not terrible. I love Mom and Dad, and it's not terrible. I even love my sneakers. And dancing. And it's not terrible. It's terrific. So if love is terrible, you're going to have to prove it to me. Except . . ." Lily stopped.

"Except what?" Saundra asked.

"Except I don't want you to prove it to me. I want you to be wrong, Saundra."

"Well, I'm *not* wrong."

"Prove it."

"Love is *terrible*," Saundra said and shut her jaws down over the words and looked at Lily in such a way that Lily felt *she* had to prove that love was *not* terrible.

"Who do you love?" Lily asked.

"Nobody!" Even the way she said it showed she was not telling the truth.

"But you told me you're in love. Are you still in love?"

"Of course I'm still in love! Do you think between this afternoon and now I could fall out of love? Do you think life is as easy as that?"

"Life is as hard as you make it."

61

"Oh, for God's sake, Lily, you sound just like Dad."

"I know it," Lily said, and she felt a smile spread over her face.

"Stop beaming!" said Saundra.

"I can't help it," Lily said. "I love Dad. Who do you love?" she repeated her earlier question.

"Nobody," Saundra said again, though now her voice was sad.

"What's this nobody's name?" Lily asked, taking a chance that Saundra wouldn't accuse her again of joking.

"Barnaby."

The sound of his name was mixed in with the sound of Saundra's tears, beginning all over again.

11
A Riddle and a Problem

The next morning, after Saundra had left the apartment for a Sunday rehearsal for *Giselle*, Lily spoke to her father about her. She always spoke to her father about problems. Or almost always. The only time she didn't was when *he* was the problem. At such times as that, she spoke to her mother about her father. But her mother always made the problem even more difficult to solve because she said that in matters involving the home and family, she simply would not pass judgment, and even to admit that someone was a problem was to pass judgment. Thus Lily had nowhere to turn when her father was the problem. It was lucky for her that he'd been a problem only about four and a half times in her whole life (the half being when he once insisted she start dancing school and took her to Capezio to buy her gear; she absolutely hated the idea and didn't want to go but ended up loving dancing and the school; so it was half a problem, otherwise known by that wonderful phrase, a blessing in disguise).

Lily found her father riding his stationary bicycle in her parents' bedroom. He used to jog to try to solve the problem of what he called his "middle riddle," which was a stomach that continued to grow, as if of its own accord, no matter what he did to make it stick in instead of out including a fast he started and then cheated on by eating everyone's toothpaste, including the spare tubes in the linen closet. He had given up jogging for several reasons: it didn't seem to solve the riddle; dogs that seemed to consider him not a man in a red jogging suit but a giant bone that went huffing and puffing around the reservoir in Central Park; boys on bikes who for one reason or another seemed to consider him invisible; and boredom. The last was the worst. He claimed he once got so bored that he fell asleep and ran around the whole reservoir snoring and woke up only when he reached out for his pillow and his pillow turned out to be a lady jogger.

Now he wasn't bored. He had rigged up a reading stand on the handlebars of his stationary bicycle, and while he pedaled he read either a book or one of his law journals. The only problem he had was when he had worked up a sweat, which caused his reading glasses to keep slipping down his nose. So he could usually be found with one hand turning a page and the other shoving his glasses back up. Unfortunately, he didn't have the greatest balance in the world. Now and then, when both hands were off the handlebars, he would fall off the bike. At such times, the whole apartment would shake. Whoever was home would stop what she was doing and listen. The next sound was always that of the shower being turned on. Lily sometimes suspected that her father fell off on purpose so he could cut short his exercise and get into the steamy water that he so loved and that turned him as pink as a baby.

When he rode, he turned redder and redder. "Red is the color of heat loss," he would say, to explain how calories got burned off and weight was lost. And maybe he did lose weight. But so far as Lily could see, what he never ever lost was a single millimeter from his middle. That particular riddle seemed beyond solving. She began to think they should put it in riddle books; it would be the only riddle without an answer in the back of the book or printed upside down at the bottom of the page.

So he was red and reading when Lily came to see him.

"I've got a problem," she said.

"Me, too," he said. That was obvious. His glasses were so far down they were resting on his upper lip. The page he was trying to read wasn't lying flat. And his sneaker was untied, which meant the lace might get caught in the chain.

"Mine has to do with Saundra," Lily said.

"Mine has to do with me," he said. "So let's start with yours."

"My problem is this," Lily said. "You love Mom, right?"

"That's a problem?" her father said. "Say, would you mind pushing up my glasses?"

Lily slid them up his wet and shiny red nose.

"Thank you," he said. "Now, as you were saying. Or as I was saying. I love your mother? The answer is yes. Now, I admit that sometimes your mother is a problem. Sometimes *I'm* a problem. . . . Well, once I was a problem. I think I was about four months old. I hiccuped while my mother was entertaining guests by singing Mozart arias with her mouth full of taffy—it was a test of her strength as well as of her voice—while my father accompanied her by tap-dancing. They said my hiccuping ruined their rhythm. The guests said my hiccuping was the prettiest sound in the room. That's probably the last time I was a problem."

Usually Lily laughed at his silly stories. But not today. "Come on, Dad. Be serious."

He looked at her. A drop of sweat hung at the end of his nose. "Oh, I see," he said. "You do look concerned. I apologize. I also quit!"

He stopped pedaling. He took the wet white towel that he kept around his neck and put it over the top of his head. It was true he looked like a red-faced, round-faced, twinkle-eyed prizefighter when he did this, but otherwise Lily couldn't figure out why someone would put a sweaty towel on top of his hair; it had to be for effect. But what effect? It must be to make people laugh, even when there were no people around to laugh. She would have loved to have laughed this time too. But she wasn't in the mood. And now that he'd stopped pedaling, she was afraid he'd rush right into the shower.

"Don't go yet," she said.

"Don't worry. It can wait." He lay down on the bed and rubbed the white towel over his hair and forehead. Then he closed his eyes. Lily was afraid he would fall asleep. But it turned out he was just thinking. For he opened his eyes and said, "What's your problem with Saundra got to do with whether I love Mom? Not a thing, I should imagine. Saundra can't be troubled these days because she might think your mother and I are getting a divorce. Lily, it would be more likely that there would be peace in every country in the world and food on every table than that we would get a divorce. I don't have to tell you that. We're stuck with one another, she and I, the way water is stuck with wetness. Speaking of water, it sure would feel good right around now—"

"Dad," Lily interrupted so he wouldn't leave for his shower, "this has nothing to do with divorce or anything. I asked you if you loved Mom so I could ask you after that if you are in love with Mom."

"What do you mean, 'in love'?"

"You know. In love."

"You mean like head over heels?"

"I guess," said Lily.

"Yeah, I know what you mean," he said, and a dreamy expression crept across his face.

"So?" she asked, getting impatient.

"Are you asking me if I'm in love with Mom?" Lily nodded.

"Why are you asking?" he said.

She knew all of a sudden that he wasn't going to answer the question. And she thought she knew why: loving and being in love were two different things, and while he loved Mom, he wasn't in love with her. He wasn't head over heels. He didn't turn cartwheels every time she came into the room . . . thank goodness.

"I'm asking because . . ." She couldn't bring herself to say it. It seemed too private, or at least too confidential.

"I think I know," he said.

"You do?"

"You're in love," he said. "You're in love, and Saundra is jealous, and her jealousy is a real problem. So she—"

"She's in love," Lily interrupted so he wouldn't go on with his mistake. "It's not me. It's her. Anyway, I'm too young."

"You *are* too young. I agree. But you kids grow up so fast these days. You never know. You just never know. Some fellow in the office, he was telling me the other day, he's got a kid, a little boy, and this kid is only seven, and the other day he told his parents that he wants to get married! He asked them to buy him and his girlfriend a house . . . a treehouse, it's true, but a house for the two of them nonetheless. Can you believe it! Seven years old, and he wants to get—"

"Dad!" Lily interrupted again. "Be serious."

"Let me finish, Lily. I'm making a point. And the point is this: it's more likely that you're in love and that this seven-year-old kid wants to get married than that Saundra is in love. I *know* Saundra. She's too closed off to be in love, she's too wrapped up in herself and her dancing, she's too *busy*.

Love takes time. It takes involvement. Saundra's involved in herself."

Lily thought for a few moments. What her father said made sense—Saundra wasn't the sort of person who got involved in anything but herself. But maybe that's what love was too—getting involved in yourself, even though you also got involved in the person you were in love with. It certainly seemed that way. Lately Saundra was even more involved in herself than usual: she hardly said anything to anyone else, her eyes and thoughts seemed turned inward, and her obvious pain seemed to come out of her from inside and then to go right back in once it had emerged.

"I know her, too," Lily said. "You're right about the kind of person she is, but she is in love. She told me so."

"She did?" her father asked, looking very surprised. "What exactly did she say?"

"She said she's in love. And that she has a broken heart."

"Well, that's just an expression. A broken heart. A lot of things can account for a broken heart. It doesn't mean she's in love. Maybe things aren't going well at the ballet. Maybe she wants a part that she's not going to get, and it's breaking her heart. Did she say anything else?"

"She said that love is terrible."

"She said that?"

Lily nodded.

"What his name?" her father asked. Now he looked worried.

"Barnaby."

12
The
Hunk

Once Lily had convinced her father that Saundra really was in love, they tried to decide what to do. The problem was not that Saundra was in love, but that she was so miserable. Had she merely been in love—mooning around the house, grinning into space for no apparent reason, even turning cartwheels in front of her beloved's photograph—then of course they wouldn't have had to do anything but simply, as Lily's father said, "let nature take its course," which Lily figured has as much to do with sex as it did with cartwheels and moons. But Saundra wasn't merely in love. She was miserably in love, unhappily, sickly, sufferingly in love. And that was why Lily and her father figured they had to do something about it.

But what? They knew hardly anything about Saundra's love. All they knew was that she had a broken heart, thought love was terrible, and was in love with nobody at all whose name happened to be Barnaby.

"Who is this Barnaby?" Lily's father asked.

Lily had no idea. She knew it was a question he was asking himself and not her, but she still felt stupid not knowing the answer.

"He's a boy." But why did she say that? What else was he supposed to be? A fish? Or a new flavor of ice cream?

"True enough," her father said. "True enough." She felt lucky that he wasn't really listening to her. At the same time, she resented it.

"We've got to find a cure," she said.

"Yes, a cure," he said. Then he looked at her. His eyes opened wide, in puzzlement. "A cure for what?"

"A cure for being in love."

"My heavens," he said. "If you find a cure for that, you'll be a rich woman. Rich and famous and they'll probably build a shrine to you and millions of people will come and visit it every year.

"Is love really that terrible?" she asked.

He put his towel over his face. Lily wondered if he were trying to hide. "I guess it can be," he said. "I don't deny it to you. Anything that can be so wonderful when it's good can be equally terrible when it's bad. And nothing can be as wonderful as love. I want you to realize that too. Nothing. But it has its price. Let me tell you, it has its price."

"And Saundra's paying it, right?" she asked.

"She certainly seems to be. And the question is, what can we do about it?"

"I think I know," said Lily.

71

He peeked out at her from behind his towel. "You do?"

"I think we should find Barnaby."

"Easier said than done," he said, replacing the towel on the top of his head. "We can't really expect Saundra to help us find him. And I'm not sure she should know we're looking. So where do we begin?"

Instead of saying where, Lily rose from where she was sitting on the bed and began to dance for her father. She went up on her toes and twirled a few times and even let her foot do a little *fouetté*, which she'd learned in yesterday's class.

He watched her impatiently, and then with puzzlement, until finally he realized what she was saying.

"Of course!" he said, smiling and reaching out to take her in his arms. "Of course! Where else? That's where you'll find this Barnaby. Go to it, Lily."

So the following Saturday she set out to find Barnaby.

She had tried to learn about him during the week from Saundra, but Saundra was almost never home, and when she was home, she was so tired from rehearsing that she ate a few nibbles of a late supper and went right to bed.

Having confessed that she was broken-heartedly in love, Saundra seemed not to want to say anything more about it at all. Lily knew she would have to work alone. It took so long for Saturday to come that she began to have her doubts that she would find Barnaby where she'd been sure, at first, that she would find him.

Needless to say, Lily thought later, considering how things in life tended to happen the opposite from how you had expected they would, Barnaby found her.

Lily was changing into her dance clothes for class when she was aware that someone—someone tall—was standing by her side. She looked up from the bench, and there, towering above her, was the most gorgeous boy she'd ever seen. He was big enough to be a man, but there was something about him, something that said he still had some growing to do and that his face wasn't yet the way it was going to be for the rest of his life, that made her think of him as a boy.

She had on only her underpants and was about to pull on her tights, but she didn't panic. This was officially the girls' dressing room, but boys often turned up unannounced and unexpectedly, usually looking for someone but sometimes just looking for a place to rest or to change their own clothes. The world of ballet was such a world of bodies, and bodies, even naked bodies, meant something so different when inside the world of ballet than when outside it that everyone was accustomed to boys and girls mixing together when their bodies were partially or even completely naked. It was no big deal. Only new kids might panic, as a few did now with this boy in the room, chirping like overexcited crickets and hurrying into their clothes so fast that both feet ended up in the same tight-leg or they stuck their heads through the armholes of their leotards and thus made matters even worse by drawing attention to themselves as they hopped around the room trying to get straightened out.

But not Lily. She just went right ahead and got into her tights, raising her behind from the bench to pull the tights over them at the same moment he spoke to her.

"Excuse me," he said. "Are you Saundra Leonard's sister?"

Now she could really look at him. He was not as tall as he'd seemed at first glance, but he was still quite big, with long, hard muscles sticking out of his skin as if they'd been blown up with a bicycle pump—dancer's muscles, because they seemed to go on forever, and didn't bulge so much as they flowed—and a head of blond hair placed like a huge and living crown atop him, drawing in the light from the room and giving off light at the same time.

Goodness, but he certainly was a prince. Even without his dance clothes on you would have known he was a dancer. His body seemed ready to leap into the air even as he stood still. His skin gave off heat and energy, and he fit into space in the most graceful possible way. He really was something, whoever he was.

Lily knew who he was.

"I'm Saundra's sister," she said. "Yes, that's who I am. Saundra's sister."

Why was it so difficult to talk to him? Why was she babbling? It couldn't be because he was so handsome. Or because she knew that this giant, golden boy held the key to Saundra's misery and Saundra's joy. It must be because what she really felt like saying was, "Hiya, you gorgeous prince of a creature, you Barnaby, you hunk."

Ugh. What flattery. It was the last thing he needed.

So she took a deep breath, looked him square in his green eyes that were as green as emeralds and as deep as outer space, and said, "What's it you to?"

Oh, God! Not only had she gotten the last two words backward, but her voice squeaked like a chipmunk's in a cartoon. She was making an utter fool of herself.

She could tell he noticed her mistake—his eyes grew dull for a moment as if to protect her from the laughter he might have laughed—but he just let it pass on by when he said, "I thought that's who you were. Lily, right?" He didn't give her time to answer. He seemed to be in a hurry, or perhaps he was just impatient with her babbling. No, he looked over his shoulder as if checking for someone he hoped wouldn't be there. "I wonder if you might do me a favor," he continued.

Now Lily waited. He was a little strange. He spoke when you didn't expect him to and fell silent when you expected him to continue speaking.

Still not trusting herself to talk, she raised her eyebrows at him.

"Oh, yes," he said. "Then you will."

Lily nodded. Then she shook her head. He smiled and then looked confused. It was her own fault. Why couldn't she say what she meant? Why couldn't she say anything at all?

"I'm sorry, but which one is it?" he asked.

Now she was caught. She would have to say

something. So, speaking very slowly and deliberately, and lowering her voice, she said, "I have to know what the favor is first." Hearing her voice, she wanted to crawl under the bench. She'd made it so low that now she sounded like a bear in a cartoon.

He stared at her and bent down a little toward her as he spoke. "Are you studying to be an actress?"

Why, what a nice thing for him to say. Maybe he was just flattering her, but if he thought she might be an actress. . . . She stuck her chin in the air and said, "No, not really. I mean, I haven't made up my mind. Why?"

"Because you use so many different voices," he said.

She wanted to put her hands over her face. He'd noticed! Oh, it was embarrassing. And yet he didn't seem to be *trying* to embarrass her. Maybe he was just trying to make her feel comfortable, by showing her that he noticed she could hardly talk.

"I *have* many different voices," she said. It was the only thing she could think of to say. And after she said it, she noticed she had spoken in what at least felt like her normal voice. She couldn't really hear it because she was trying to be deaf to herself in case her voice came out upside down or something equally as ridiculous.

"Hey, I know what you mean," he said. "So do I. Sometimes when I'm alone I find myself talking to myself in a voice so high I sound like a chipmunk. You know, one of those chipmunks who used to be on those records. . . ." He squinted as he tried to think of the name, but he couldn't and shook his head.

That was all right. What was really amazing was that both of them had thought of chipmunks when they thought of high, squeaky voices. For the first time since she had sensed his presence next to her, Lily felt at least slightly comfortable. Their minds seemed to work in the same way. It was a very good sign.

"About the favor . . ," Lily said. And she realized she was leading the conversation for the first time. It felt good.

"Oh, sure," he said. "Anything you say."

Anything she said! He must have forgotten he'd asked *her* for a favor. She had so captivated him that he was willing to do a favor for her, any favor.

Quick. What should she ask him for?

Take me in your arms, you hunk, and dance me around the room. . . . No no no no no. She must not be selfish. It was Saundra she had to think of now.

"My sister . . ." she began, and through her mind went words like *is in love with you . . . please take her out of her misery . . . she's really a great person once you get to know her for about ten years . . . is printed indelibly on the film of your consciousness, naked . . .*

"What's the matter?" he asked.

What made him think anything was the matter? She tried to speak, but all that came out was "Huh?"

"Your face is all red."

That was all she needed. Whenever someone told her she was blushing, she blushed.

Her face turned on like a microwave. But she didn't hide it. She looked right into those swimming-pool eyes of his and said, "What does her body do to you?"

She didn't really want him to tell her. She hadn't even wanted Saundra to tell her. She just wanted to see what would happen if she asked.

What happened was perfect. Barnaby turned bright red and shook his head from side to side as if he wished his hair could cover his face, and then, when he tried to speak, he just ended up clearing his throat several times in a row.

Lily was enjoying this immensely. Here he was, the most gorgeous hunk of guy-creature on earth—or at least in the girls' dressing room at that moment—and he was matching her in the crimson-skin department.

"Are you crazy, Lily?" he said finally. "What my . . . my body does? Why my body does to someone? What has that got to do with the price of eggs? I mean . . . Oh, God, you've got me all flustered."

Lily didn't really want him to feel uncomfortable and unable to say what he meant, but she loved it that he did. She felt like a princess herself, next to her flustered prince, even though she knew she'd gotten to feel like one in the wrong way, by confusing him with her wicked, wicked tongue.

But she couldn't stop herself. "Tell me," she asked, "are you studying to be an actor?"

He looked at her as if he couldn't believe her and then seemed to look back at himself as if he couldn't believe what was about to burst forth from him once he stopped holding his breath. It was a funny little giggle, like a little boy's. But his green eyes swam with older laughter and his ridiculously white teeth seemed about to dance, so cheerful was his smile.

He opened his mouth to say something, but what they both heard was his own name.

"BARNABY!"

Both he and Lily looked toward the sound. It came from just outside the door to the dressing room. It came from the large open mouth of Meredith Meredith. She was standing in the doorway, fists on her hips, glaring at the two of them.

Lily could hear Barnaby gasp. Then he turned to go. But before he left he took her hand and held it. A thrill went through her. So did a terrible feeling of responsibility: when he took his hand away, she found her own holding a piece of paper.

"For Saundra," he whispered. And then Lily understood what he had wanted of her.

13
Love's Detective

It was a note for Saundra. Her name was written on the outside of it. But only her name. Not "Personal and Confidential," as on the outside of certain memos her father brought home from the office. Barnaby's note said merely, SAUNDRA. And it was just a piece of paper folded over, without even a paper clip or tape holding it together. There was nothing to stop her from reading it.

It was probably important for her to read it. If it said, "I love you. Yours forever, Barnaby," then she'd have to find Saundra immediately and make her stop whatever she was doing and show it to her and cure her instantly of her broken heart.

But if it said, "I don't love you. Yours never, Barnaby," then maybe she should rip it up. A broken heart was one thing. But a heart that disappeared was another. And Lily was afraid that

Saundra's heart was in the process of disappearing, or at least of freezing up, which was probably even worse.

And in a way, the note *was* her business. Her parents had sent her out to learn what was the matter with Saundra. She was love's detective. But she knew from reading mysteries that even detectives weren't supposed to break the law. And the law was quite simple: don't read other people's notes.

There were two things she could hope for.

One was to find Saundra immediately, give Saundra the note, and hope that Saundra would tell her what it said.

That was the most practical thing. So Lily rushed into her dancing clothes so quickly that, like a mere beginner or like someone who was afraid of being seen naked, she put both feet into one tight-leg and then put her head into an armhole of her leotard. It took her longer to get dressed than it usually did.

The second thing was not so practical. The second thing she hoped for was that someone would send her a note. Someone who was a gorgeous hunk like Barnaby. The note would say LILY on the outside, and she would be free to open it and read it. And no matter what it said, it would be said to her and her alone.

She knew she was already late for class and would be even later if she tried to find Saundra. Miss Witt would have a fit, as the kids in the class like to rhyme. Well, let her. It was more important that Saundra got to read her note and maybe find comfort in it than that Lily try the hopeless task of mastering the *fouetté rond de jambe en tournant,* which she could hardly pronounce, let alone do. And she wasn't sure she wanted to be able to do turns around a room on one leg while whipping herself along with the other. It looked nice when someone like Saundra did it. But when Lily and the other kids in her class tried it, they ended up kicking each other or themselves with the whipping foot, losing their balance, sometimes falling down, and finally just getting silly and giggling, until Miss Witt screamed, "Sil*ence!*" pronouncing it in French—"See-*lawnce!*"—and stamped her tiny foot on the floor. That was it. The next kid who talked or giggled got humiliated personally by Miss Witt.

There was no question about it: delivering the note was more important than *fouetté*ing clumsily around a room and ending up getting screamed at by a strange little woman who never danced.

So Lily took the note and went out into the hallway and brushed past various students coming from class and going to class, and she climbed the stairs, not exactly sure where she'd find Saundra but certain that it would be up toward the top of the building, where those who were members of one of the American Ballet Center's two companies often practiced and rehearsed and isolated themselves from the rest of the school.

She'd never been above the fourth floor before, and wasn't even sure you could get beyond it. But, after looking in three practice rooms and not finding Saundra, she located a door that opened onto a stairway that took her up past the fourth floor.

She could hear piano music and the pounding of feet. They got louder and louder as she climbed.

Two floors up beyond the closed door, she entered a room that stretched from one side of the building to the other. It took up the entire top floor of the American Ballet Center. And it was filled with dancers. They were in various groups and were being instructed by various teachers. Some were dancing and others were listening. It seemed like a chaos, but Lily knew that this was the way a ballet was put together, piece by piece, group by group, dancer by dancer, step by step. You didn't rehearse the dance the way it was danced when it was one piece. You rehearsed it by moments. You pulled it apart and looked at it and tested it and even changed it. You *built* it.

She was just thinking of the name of the ballet when she heard her own name.

"Lily! Lily, what are you doing here?"

It was Saundra. She was sweating and had a bandanna tied around her neck to catch some of the sweat. On her wrists were sweatbands—and it was just like Saundra that they matched the color of her bandanna. Black. She was wreathed in black, her sad sister.

But she was also angry. Her eyes were fierce. They were pushing Lily from the room, where she had no business being.

It was now or never.

"Here," said Lily.

"What's that?" said Saundra, not reaching for it.

"A note."

"What does it say?"

"I didn't read it."

Saundra looked surprised. "Why not?"

"I don't read other people's mail. I wanted to, but I didn't."

"I would have," said Saundra. "Look, it's not even sealed. I would have read it in a second."

"Well, I guess we're different."

"Yeah," said Saundra. "I don't even want to read it."

"I don't believe you."

"It's probably just a fan note from one of the girls. Sucking up to me. Wanting to bask in my glory."

This was Saundra at her most haughty. But Lily could tell she was acting. Her nose was not stuck in the air. In fact, her head was bent down as her eyes tried to see into the fold of the note.

"So who's it from?" Saundra asked as if she couldn't care less. "Some girl? Or one of those dumb boys who are always trying to get into my leos, those stupid, dumb, ugly boys who—"

Lily couldn't stand it any longer. She no longer cared if Saundra ever read the note. But she was still dying to know what was in it herself. And the only way she was going to learn was to get Saundra to read it.

"A boy," she said.

"What did he—"

"He's a real hunk, Saundra. A real hunk. Tall as a tree and blond hair and green eyes and muscles like—"

"Barnaby!" Saundra whispered and screeched

at the same time. The sound hurt Lily's ear. But the pain in her hand was worse. Saundra grabbed for the note and scratched Lily as she pulled it away. And at that Saundra got only half the note. Lily was still holding the other half, in her wounded hand.

"Gimme," said Saundra, grabbing for the other half while her desperate eyes were already reading the half she had.

Lily hurriedly handed over her half, to avoid being scratched again.

Saundra put the two halves of the note together about three times until she got them right. Then she stood there completely still, not even breathing, her eyes moving up and down, up and down, the little piece of paper.

When her eyes left the note, they didn't go where Lily had expected them to go, which was toward Lily's own eyes. They went instead up to the ceiling, which had a large skylight. It was as if Saundra were looking right up to heaven when she said, "There's hope. There's hope."

Lily reached out for the note, but instead of giving it to her, Saundra folded it up and put it gently into her leotard between her breasts. Then she merely turned around and rejoined her group of dancers.

Lily couldn't believe it. All that trouble, and she still didn't know what the note said. What a waste of time. She should have given it to the mailman.

Feeling useless and cheated, she left the room and started down the stairs, wondering in her mind what Miss Witt would say to humiliate her personally. All sorts of insults were occurring to her and, strangely, making her smile when she nearly bumped into a statue of two people kissing. What a strange place for a statue, in the almost secret stairway above the fourth floor in the American Ballet Center. Except it wasn't a statue. It was alive.

It was Meredith Meredith and Barnaby, so involved with one another's lips that they didn't even notice Lily as she crept by them on the stairs. Also aiding her escape, she realized, was the fact that in real life just as in the movies, people kissing like there was no tomorrow kept their eyes closed so they wouldn't see the world or time going by.

She didn't breathe until she was on the fourth floor and had closed the stairway door behind her. And it was then that it occurred to her for the first time that whatever hope Saundra saw looked pretty hopeless.

14
A
Curse
in
Disguise

Lily missed a good half of her class. When Miss Witt saw her entering late, she humiliated her by stopping the lesson and pretending Lily had been there all along.

"Now, to demonstrate," said Miss Witt, "I call on Curly. Curly." Miss Witt gestured for Lily to come to the center of the floor. Lily walked slowly out from among the other girls and boys, not particularly nervous or concerned because she was still thinking about Saundra and that hopeless, hopeful note. Besides, no matter what Miss Witt asked her to do, she knew she wasn't going to be able to do it. She knew Miss Witt well enough to know that.

"Curly, will you be so kind as to give us a *fouetté en dedans* in the Cecchetti method." Her voice was softer than usual, but the moment she finished speaking, she slapped her hands together as if a mosquito the size of a bulldog had just buzzed her nose. Practically everyone in the class jumped at the sound. Miss Witt wasn't fooling around.

Lily knew she couldn't do what Miss Witt had asked. She didn't even know what Miss Witt was asking her to do. But instead of moving her body around in pretense the way some kids did when they had been singled out for personal humiliation, Lily just stood completely still and looked at Miss Witt as if she didn't know what she was talking about. Lily felt this was the proper thing to do, because she *didn't* know what Miss Witt was talking about.

Lily thought this was how Saundra would handle the situation, haughty and still and staring straight ahead . . . and inside shaking like a leaf.

Miss Witt's eyes burned as they looked at Lily. But her voice was only a bit louder than when she'd issued her first request.

"If you don't mind, Curly, do, please, do what I asked. If perhaps you've forgotten the instructions, let me refresh your memory. Give me a *pirouette en dedans* and then immediately extend your working leg to the fourth position *derrière en l'air*. Then a *demi-rond de jambe en l'air en dedans*, so the foot is brought right to the front of the other knee. Am I understood? So!" This time she clapped her hands so loud that one of the girls, who must have been daydreaming, shrieked at the sound. "So, Curly?" Miss Witt said threateningly, smiling for the first time, probably, Lily figured, because she'd made the other girl scream, though it might be because she knew that Lily couldn't possibly do what she'd asked. "Wellll?" Miss Witt prompted.

How was she going to get out of this one?

Then she had it all figured out.

"Miss Witt," she said in a voice she tried to make sound sweet and humble, "would you please demonstrate it for me."

Miss Witt's mouth fell open and at the same time her eyes narrowed into slits; then her eyes opened wide and her mouth closed and she held her lips so tight they looked like barbed wire. It was as if her mouth and her eyes were connected by strings. Miss Witt was trying to look mean, but all Lily could see was a dummy whose mouth and eyes were coordinated nonsensically.

Lily smiled. She smiled to keep from bursting into laughter. Sometimes you could do that.

"Please," she said.

Miss Witt raised a hand and started to point a finger toward the person who was in charge of demonstrating. "Mrs. Howell—" she began.

"No, *you*," Lilly interrupted. "You demonstrate it for me, please, Miss Witt."

No one had ever seen Miss Witt dance. Or do a single step, for that matter. There were all sorts of rumors about her, including one that said she used to be one of the greatest ballerinas in the world and another that said she had never danced a step in her life. Lily had once asked her father about this, and he had said that a great teacher did not have to be able to do what she was teaching. Some people, he said, were blessed with the ability to teach. And while this was a blessing for their students, it might be a curse for them, because if they wanted to be able to do what they taught other people to do but couldn't do themselves, then they would live a life of terrible frustration. And Lily thought that just as there were blessings in disguise, so there must be curses in disguise.

Poor Miss Witt. She was standing there unable to move, except for her lips, which twitched sharply but said nothing.

The room was terribly quiet. No one spoke or moved. Everyone was waiting for Miss Witt to prove herself.

Poor Miss Witt. A *demi-rond de jambe en l'air en dedans*. She did not know how to do it. Or she couldn't do it. It didn't matter. It was her pupils' thing to do. And Lily was her pupil. And she couldn't do it. Suddenly Lily felt ashamed.

She had failed her teacher. She had failed herself. The only thing she'd done was to humiliate Miss Witt personally. And it wasn't right to do it. Even if Miss Witt had tried to humiliate *her*. What she should have done was a *demi-rond de jambe en l'air en dedans*. Then neither one of them would have been humiliated.

"I'm sorry," Lily said softly to Miss Witt. "I'm sorry I was late. I'm sorry I don't know how to do the *demi-rond* thing. I had a lot on my mind. My sister—"

"No excuses," whispered Miss Witt, as if she didn't want anyone else to hear. Then she moved her lips in what Lily imagined was Miss Witt's way of smiling: they didn't turn up at the corners, nor did they wiggle around like Meredith Meredith's, but at least they relaxed enough to open up and show the tip of her pink tongue, and Lily knew it was a sign of some kind of pleasure and relief. "And it's not a *demi-rond* thing. It's a *demi-rond de jambe en l'air en dedans*." She was still speaking softly, but even so, she bent forward to put her mouth right next to Lily's ear. Lily bent forward too. She knew Miss Witt didn't want a soul to hear. "It only *sounds* difficult," Miss Witt said. "It's really not so hard, even if it is in fourth position. You're one of my best pupils. You're conscientious. You'll be able to do it. I know you will, Curly." And then she touched her lips to Lily's ear and held them there and said. "I know you will, Lily."

It was the first time Miss Witt had ever called her by her real name. Lily felt like kissing her. But as the warm surprise flowed through Lily from her feet right up through her curly hair, Miss Witt almost ran backward in her short little steps, assumed her usual position on the stool against the mirrored wall, clapped her hands so loud that it might have been an elephant zeroing in on her nose, and screamed, "Better late than never, class. Better late than never. Am I understood? To the *barre*, then. To the *barre!*"

Later everyone congratulated Lily. "You really got back at her," they said. "You gave it to her good." "I thought she was going to bite off your ear." "No one ever put her in her place before." "Phooey on her *fouetté*." And the girl who considered herself the brain in the class and also thought she was a terrific dancer, though Lily knew that if she had a brain at all it was in her big toe, said, "Now that's what I call a comeuppance!"

Lily said nothing in return and got dressed as quickly as possible. It hadn't been right to make a fool of Miss Witt in front of her pupils, even if she deserved it. Because Miss Witt was such a good teacher. She was hard on her pupils, but she was harder on herself. She didn't disguise her feelings, except maybe when she was whispering something nice in your ear. And she had more to teach you than you had to teach her. Lily believed this, though she had a feeling that Miss Witt had learned something today, if only that Lily Leonard was a tough little kid.

Lily had no desire to bask in the glory of her confrontation. So what if she could intimidate practically anyone? She had a far tougher case to solve.

She had to save her sister from a hopeless situation.

15

Favorite
Books

This was one time Lily didn't want to go home with Saundra. Usually she dressed very slowly in the hope that her sister's class or rehearsal would end in time for them to leave together. She knew that often Saundra wanted to be alone after dancing—Saundra told her that she was mentally and physically exhausted, "empty." Lily would say that she understood, that expressing yourself in your art could leave you this way, and that what she wanted from Saundra at such times was nothing more than to be with her. Saundra would nod and often not say a word the whole way home. But Lily would talk anyway and be quite content just trying to feel how Saundra felt and wondering what it was like to have found something in life into which you threw so much of yourself that there was nothing left over for anything or anyone else.

Now Lily wasn't sure that this was the case. If

Saundra was in love—and she said she was and was acting as if she was—then her whole life must be changing. She loved dancing, although sometimes she hated it. But if she also loved Barnaby, then she was going to have to learn to throw herself into *more* than one thing, into two things, and to have something left after each of them for the other. How could Saundra do this? She had no practice. Her whole life had been the dance.

And to make matters worse, she had a broken heart. It was obvious to Lily that Saundra loved Barnaby. It was also obvious that Saundra didn't know whether Barnaby loved her. It was obvious to Lily that Barnaby loved to kiss Meredith Meredith, so that must mean he loved her, because, boy, they were really kissing! And if Barnaby loved Meredith Meredith, then how could he love Saundra at the same time?

To make matters even worse than that—and they really did look pretty hopeless—Meredith Meredith must have known that Saundra loved Barnaby because she had told Lily to tell Saundra that she didn't have a chance. What else could it mean? Saundra didn't have a chance to win Barnaby because Meredith Meredith had won Barnaby. Of course, the last time Meredith Meredith had told Lily to tell Saundra she didn't have a chance at something, Meredith Meredith had been wrong, because Saundra had gone on to win the audition, after Lily had intimidated Meredith Meredith. But winning an audition couldn't be the same as winning a boyfriend. One was mostly a matter of how well you could dance. The other was mostly a

matter of how well you could . . . what? Smile?
Look pretty? Whisper sweet nothings? Kiss?

Whatever it was, it wasn't an audition. And
Saundra couldn't win Barnaby by having Lily intimidate Meredith Meredith. Could she?

Lily had to get out of there before Saundra
came down from her rehearsal. There was so much
to think about.

She had to find out what was in that note.
What could it be that was hopeful in a situation
that looked so hopeless? She had to figure out
what to do about Meredith Meredith. And she
needed some time to talk to the only other friends
that Saundra seemed to have in the world, who
were as worried about her as Lily was.

Her parents were in their bathrobes when
she got home. Whenever she really rushed home
after class, they seemed to be in their bathrobes.
Whenever she waited for Saundra and they took
their time getting home, her parents were dressed
for whatever they were planning to do on Saturday
night. Lily figured they had it timed pretty well,
except that they always expected Lily and Saundra
to come home together, since that was what they
usually did. When they didn't, she found her parents in their bathrobes, and embarrassed.

Today, as always, they made their usual excuses.

"You get to be our age you need a nap, huh,
Judge?" her father asked her mother.

"Oh, yes," said her mother. "I always feel
good after a nap."

Her father winked at her mother. "I feel better than good. I feel terrific!"

"That's nothing compared to how I feel," said her mother. "I feel . . ." She hesitated and started to giggle.

"*How* do you feel?" asked her husband. He winked at her again. Then he started to giggle too.

Lily loved to see them this way. It was always nice when you realized your parents actually had fun together and didn't spend all their time just working and trying to raise their kids to be serious people who didn't swear much and didn't shoplift ever and would never smoke or be prejudiced or mug people or run away from home before it was time to leave for college.

At the same time, Lily sometimes got annoyed at them when they behaved this way. Fun was fine, but she didn't like it when they acted embarrassed, as if they'd done something to be ashamed of, and they had to pretend they'd been napping when actually they'd been having sex. Napping! So far as she was concerned, she'd be more embarrassed to say she was napping than to say she'd been having sex. At least it seemed that way now. Maybe after she'd had sex she would change her mind. But she doubted it.

To make her parents stop laughing, she said, "Caught in the act."

It didn't make them stop immediately, but at least they let go of one another and looked at her and quieted down.

"What act?" asked her father.

"You know," said Lily.

"What act?" her mother asked also.

"Don't make me say it," Lily answered.

"We don't mind," said her father. "Go ahead and say it."

"Oh, no," said her mother to her father. And to Lily she said, "You don't have to say anything."

"That's the judge speaking," said Lily's father. "Anything you say may be held against you."

"That's right," said Lily's mother to her father, pretending to be stern. "And that goes for you too."

"I wasn't going to say anything," he said. "Lily was going to say something. Weren't you, Lily?"

"Yup," she said.

"What?" he asked.

"I was going to say that I'm glad you two get a chance to fool around."

"Fool around?" her father questioned.

"You know," said Lily.

"Oh, I most certainly do," said her father.

"Harold, really!" said his wife.

"The kid's no dope, Judge," he said, and he put his hand into Lily's curly hair.

"Don't touch the merchandise," she said. She always said that when he put his hand on her head. They both knew she meant just the opposite.

"Whatever you say," he said and put the other hand there, too. "Now, what's on your mind?"

"Who said anything was on my mind?"

"Where are my hands?" he asked.

"On my head."

"Right. So don't tell me you don't have something on your mind. I can feel it right here." He pulled his hands away and held them out for her to see.

"You can feel my thoughts?"

"I can," he said. "And I can read them, too.

Right on your pretty face and in your worried eyes."

"Is it that obvious?" Lily asked.

"No," he said. "I don't suppose most people would see it. But parents are special readers."

"Am I your favorite book?" she asked.

"You're one of them," he said.

"And we have only two," said her mother.

"Well," said Lily, "your other favorite book doesn't have a very happy story."

They both looked right at her. They were serious now.

"Tell it to us anyway," her father said.

And Lily did.

She told them all about getting a note for Saundra from that gorgeous hunk Barnaby, who snuck it to her so Meredith Meredith wouldn't see; about giving it to Saundra, who seemed to find hope in it; and then about seeing Barnaby and Meredith Meredith absolutely feasting on each other's lips in the stairway.

"Wow!" said her father.

"Poor Saundra," said her mother.

"Poor Barnaby," said Lily, surprising them both.

"Why 'poor Barnaby'?" asked her mother.

"How would *you* like to be kissed on the lips by Meredith Meredith? Ugh!"

"It doesn't seem to bother Barnaby," said her father.

"But what I don't understand," said her mother, "is why Barnaby can kiss Meredith Meredith one minute and send love notes to Saundra the next."

"Because he's a boy," said her husband.

"Who said it was a love note?" said Lily.

This was a mystery they all felt had to be solved, and as soon as possible: the mystery of Barnaby's note. If Barnaby held the key to Saundra's happinesss, then Barnaby's note might hold the key to what chance Saundra had to win Barnaby. They had to find out what was in the note.

But how?

"She'll never tell us," Lily's mother said.

"And we'll probably never get to see the note," her father added. "She'll most likely get rid of it, she's so private about these things."

Lily thought for a moment and then said, "You're both wrong."

They both looked at her.

"She won't tell us just like that," Lily said. "She won't tell us right out of the blue. But if we ask, she might tell us. If we ask in the right way. Also, I know she didn't get rid of the note."

"Why?" her father asked. "Did you see her put it somewhere?"

Lily pretended she had on a leotard and opened it with one hand and put a finger down her chest with the other.

"What does that have to do with it?" her father asked.

"Oh, Harold, don't you understand?" said his wife. "Really, you don't know women very well. I know exactly what Lily means."

"The note got stuck in her shirt?" her father joked.

"Silly," said her mother affectionately.

"She'll never throw that note away," Lily said. "Not ever. That's what I meant."

"How do you know?" her father asked.

"It means too much to her," Lily answered. "It means everything."

"It seems to be all she has," said her mother.

"But what does it *say*?" her father asked.

"That's what we have to find out," her mother said. "But how?"

They both looked at Lily. She knew what they wanted. She had known it all along.

"Don't worry," she said. "I'll find out."

Her parents seemed relieved. They smiled at each other and then at her. She tried to smile back but couldn't. She'd found out what had been making Saundra so miserable. Now, she realized, she had to find the cure for a broken heart.

16
The
Note

Saundra was pouty. Lily was anxious. But she knew she had to wait until her parents had gone out for the evening. It was something fancy. Their mother wore a long gown, their father wore his tuxedo. "I was married in this tux," he always said when he put it on. This was to excuse the fact that it was so small around the waist that he couldn't fasten the button but had to hold the pants together with a giant safety pin. But what no one could figure out was why the pants were so short; they came up to the top of his socks. He claimed he'd gotten taller since he was married, but they all said that was impossible. "You don't understand," he'd answer. "As soon as the Judge said, 'I do,' I was so proud of myself that I grew three inches." He'd wait for his wife to blush and smile, which she always did. Then he'd add: "Either that, or my pants shrank." And everyone would laugh.

But nothing her mother could say would shame him into buying a new tuxedo. Lily figured the real reason was that he *had* been married in this one, and every time he went out on the town wearing it, he remembered his wedding and was happy.

Tonight they were going to a charity ball.

"If they'd let me stay home with you guys," he told Lily and Saundra, "I'd contribute double."

"What's it for?" Lily asked.

"Save the Frogs," her father said.

Lily laughed.

"I'm not kidding," he said. "Someone found out that the pollution is wiping out all the frogs in the city. And a city without frogs is like a hospital without patients."

"I don't get it," Lily said.

"No one's croaking," he replied.

Even Saundra, who had uttered hardly a word since she'd come home from rehearsal, said, "Ugh."

Their father hung his head because his joke had been so terrible. Then he raised it. He was smiling again.

"Well, it's not as bad as the last ball," he said.

"What was that one for?" Lily said, knowing she was, as usual, feeding him what he called his lines.

"That one was for Yours Truly."

"For *you*?" Lily asked.

"No, for Yours Truly," he said. "It's a new kind of deodorant."

"I've never heard of it," said Saundra, who was interested in things like deodorants and new kinds of soaps that were guaranteed to make you smell like an orchard at dawn on a sunny day and perfumes that cost a fortune but always came with a free travel bag that had some man's initials on it.

"Of course you've never heard of it," said their father. "They gave away free samples of it that night, and everyone sprayed it on everyone else, and the smell was so bad we had to evacuate the ballroom." He laughed.

"You make me sick with your ridiculous jokes," said Saundra, who turned abruptly and walked out of the living room and toward the back of the apartment where her bedroom was.

Lily looked at her father. His face was sad. She knew his sadness didn't come from the criticism of his jokes. He was used to that from Saundra and even from the Judge. His sadness, Lily knew, came from trying to make Saundra feel better, and not succeeding.

"You've got to help her," he said to Lily. "She won't talk to us. She won't even listen to us. She's at that age. Hell, she's always been at that age. Poor Saundra." He tugged at his waist. "God, I hate this tuxedo. I'm getting fat. The ball's in your court. Bye, kiddo."

He touched her cheek and walked toward where the Judge was waiting at the front door. The Judge must have been able to see from his expression how he was feeling because she touched his cheek, too. With the other hand she waved forlornly at Lily, who waited until they had closed the door behind them to take a deep breath, which she held until she found Saundra in their bedroom.

Saundra was sitting on her bed, and whatever she had been doing when Lily walked in, she pretended she hadn't been doing. Lily saw Saundra hide something under her behind and then sit up so straight that it looked too rigid even for Saundra, who was famous for having a spine like a steel rod and always made everyone around her feel they had the posture of a thousand-year-old dachshund.

Lily decided the best approach was a direct one.

"What does it say?" she asked.

"What does what say?"

"What you're sitting on."

"My bed?"

"The note."

"What note?"

"The note I gave you today. The note from Barnaby. The note that gave you hope."

"I'm not sitting on any note."

"Get up then."

"I will *not!*" Saundra said angrily. "Don't you tell me what to do. Why don't you mind your own business. Leave me alone. Get out of here. You make me sick with your—"

Lily jumped. She left both her feet and went up into the air and came down with her head in Saundra's stomach and her hands around her back. Saundra screamed and tried to push Lily off, but as strong as Saundra was from her dancing and her eternal exercising, Lily held on and pushed with her knees against the mattress until Saundra rolled over and Lily let go with one of her hands and felt around on the bed until she found the piece of paper. Then she leaned to the side and toppled off Saundra and ended up lying beside her.

Saundra grabbed for the note, but Lily moved it out of her reach.

"That's mine!" said Saundra. "You have no right—"

"I want your permission to read it," Lily interrupted.

"You *what*!"

"You heard me. I want—"

"You have the nerve to jump on me from across the room and fight with me over a silly piece of paper and *steal* it from me, and then you ask for my permission to read it. After what you just did, I'm surprised you don't just run away with it and broadcast it all over the neighborhood."

"I'm sorry I had to get it this way," said Lily. "May I have your permission to read it?"

"You may not!"

"Then here." Lily stuck out her hand with the taped-together note and moved it toward Saundra. Saundra reached out for the note and seemed about to take it when her fingers started to tremble and her eyelids to twitch and her lips to shake. It was never easy for Saundra to cry. Her whole body seemed to have to get involved before the tears would come. And sometimes they never did, anyway. But this time they broke through. Little drops of water made her lashes glisten and then slid down her cheeks and fell on her outstretched arm.

"Read it, Lily," she said, with sobs breaking through the words. "Please. It's all right. Read it. Tell me what to do. Tell me what I can do."

Lily read the note. Then she read it again. She looked at Saundra, who was still crying but was looking intently at her all the while. Then Lily read it again.

"I don't get it," Lily said. "I don't get it at all. What does it mean?"

"I don't know," Saundra wailed.

"Then why did you say, 'There's hope, there's hope'?"

"Because he wrote me a note."

"You mean, that's all?" asked Lilly. "Just because he wrote you a note? You don't care what the note says?"

"Of course I care what the note says. But any note is better than no note. Besides, it says he loves me."

Lily read the note again. Shaking her head, she said, "It does and it doesn't. It doesn't say, 'I love you.' "

"But it uses the word *love*."

"You mean because it's signed 'Love, Barnaby'?" asked Lily. "But some people put 'love' at the end of a letter the way other people put 'sincerely.' It's just a way of saying the letter's over and goodbye. It doesn't mean they're sincere. And it doesn't mean they're in love."

"Then why would he say, 'Love, Barnaby'? Especially after—"

"That's what *I* can't figure out," Lily interrupted. "Why would he say, 'Love, Barnaby,' after he wrote a note that says, 'Leave me alone. You don't have a chance'?"

When Saundra actually heard the words of the note said aloud, she started to cry all over again.

Lily put down the piece of paper and opened up

her arms and reached out for her sister, who hesitated a moment and then forgot about her perfect posture and fell all huddled up and weak with sadness into Lily's comforting grasp.

Even so defeated, Saundra felt strong to Lily, strong and big. But she was her big sister, after all, older and more mature, in her teens and well on her way to becoming a woman—people even called her "young woman," while they still called Lily "little girl." And so it would have been more normal for Saundra to be holding Lily like this, taking care of her and drying her tears. But Saundra had never really done that, and Lily had never really needed it. It wasn't that she didn't get sad and cry. But somehow she always seemed to get over it by herself. Maybe there was something about being a child that protected you like a shield against the sort of suffering Saundra was going through. Saundra's shield might have been lost, or shattered, or taken away, for no other reason than that she was becoming a woman. It's enough to make you want to stay a child forever, thought Lily.

But there had to be more to it than that, or less. Growing up and growing older should be a positive thing. She refused to believe that the worst was yet to come, refused to believe the evidence of Saundra's sadness and, as she held her, vowed to make it go away by getting to the heart of this mystery.

17

From Afar

One thing that there had to be more to, or less than, was the note. It just didn't make sense. You didn't tell someone you were sick of her and to leave you alone and that she didn't have a chance—you weren't so mean and nasty—and then sign "Love" next to your name. It was what her father called a "mixed message."

She said exactly this to Saundra, after she had dried her tears and recovered her composure and was sitting up once again all by herself with that beautifully disdainful posture of hers.

"I think Barnaby's giving you a mixed message," Lily said.

"What do you mean by that?"

"The note. It says he hates you and it says he loves you. That's a mixed message."

"It only looks mixed," said Saundra. "He probably doesn't hate me, but I know he doesn't love me. The only thing he loves is himself. You saw him. He's gorgeous! Men are so terrible. So vain. He thinks just because he looks like that he can go around breaking people's hearts. He's in love with *himself*. He's too beautiful to let himself be in love with anyone else. He's awful. I hate him."

"Gee, I thought he was nice," said Lily. "And talk about mixed messages. You say he broke your heart, which must mean you love him, and yet you say you hate him. You're just like him. Love and hate at the same time. Anyway, you're just as beautiful as he is, and you let *your*self be in love with someone else."

Saundra sat up even straighter. "I am?"

"Just as beautiful," Lily said, knowing it to be true but admitting it at this moment only because she wanted to give Saundra as much confidence as possible for the struggle ahead.

"Then why doesn't he love me *back*?" Saundra snapped.

"Maybe he does," said Lily. "But it wouldn't be just because you're beautiful. At least I hope not. It's one thing to think someone looks good. But that's not a reason to love her. What if someone's ugly? Is that a reason *not* to love her?"

"You're asking the wrong person," Saundra admitted, sticking her chin in the air so her long neck showed in all its perfection.

"I should have known," said Lily.

"Can I help it if I'm beautiful?" Saundra said. "A lot of good it's doing me. It's making me even more miserable than if I were ugly. If I were ugly, I could understand why he doesn't love me. This way, I know it's true, but I don't understand it. How do you think that makes me feel?"

"Confused?"

"Horrible! It makes me feel like there must be something horribly wrong with me if I can look like this and he still doesn't love me. And I love *him*. *That's* the worst thing of all. I'd give him anything, I'd do anything for him, and he tells me to leave him alone. He tells me he's sick of me. It doesn't even sound like him."

"It doesn't sound like him?" Lily asked.

"No, it doesn't," Saundra replied. Then her eyes opened wide and her mouth went loose and she got a dreamy expression on her face. "He's usually very sweet. He's kind of quiet and even shy, and he has only nice things to say about people, and his voice is soft, and when he talks he makes me feel—"

"It doesn't sound like him?" Lily asked again .

Saundra didn't like being jolted out of her reverie. "I told you it doesn't! If you aren't going to listen to me when I tell you something . . ."

Saundra stopped. Lily figured Saundra must have noticed she was suddenly thinking like a demon.

"It doesn't sound like him?" she repeated.

"For God's *sake*, Lily! How many times—"

"I've got it!"

"What?" Saundra stuck her face up in the air, pretending not to be interested, but the whole rest of her body leaned toward Lily on the bed.

"Barnaby didn't write the note," she said.

Saundra looked at her as if she were crazy. "Oh, don't be silly. It's his handwriting. Of course he wrote the note. What do you think, he got his mother to—"

"I'm not talking about his handwriting," Lily said. "But how do you know what his handwriting looks like, anyway? Have you received other notes from him that you haven't told me about?"

Saundra looked down toward her beautifully ugly feet on the bed and blushed as much as it was possible for her to blush: the very tip of her nose turned a strange orange at the same time that her cheeks got very pale because she was sucking them in against her teeth. This is how she always looked when she got caught at something.

"Well?" prompted Lily, when Saundra said nothing.

"No, I didn't get another note from him. I only wish I had.".

"So how do you know his handwriting?"

"I snuck a look at it, if you have to know."

"Where?" asked Lily. "Did he write your name all over his leotard?"

Saundra looked as if she might cry again. "That's a rotten thing to say," she said.

Lily felt bad. Saundra was right. "I'm sorry," she apologized. "But it's very frustrating talking to you sometimes. Sometimes you don't tell me anything and it's like pulling strings."

"Pulling teeth, Lily. The expression is, pulling teeth. And what do you expect me to say? That I know his handwriting because one day I left rehearsal and found his wallet in his pants in the dressing room and looked in his wallet and saw his handwriting and a whole lot more?"

"That's terrible," said Lily.

"I know it's terrible. But that's how desperate I am. When your heart is broken, you'll—"

"Saundra," Lily interrupted, feeling that this was not the time for talk of broken hearts as much as it was time to begin to solve the mystery of the broken heart. "Saundra, I'm sorry I said it was terrible. I'm sorry I said did he write your name all over his leotard. I'm even sorry I asked you about his handwriting, because I don't care about his handwriting. What I care about is—"

"But didn't you say he didn't write the note?" Saundra asked.

"I did," said Lily. "But I didn't mean *write* the note." She scribbled in the air with her hand. "I didn't mean he didn't write it. I meant he didn't *write* it."

"What do you *mean*?" Saundra screamed.

Lily felt like a great detective. She knew exactly what she meant and was about to reveal the answer, but in the meantime, everyone around her was going nuts with curiosity.

"Let me put it this way, my dear Saundra," she said, pretending to be Basil Rathbone as Sherlock Holmes. "Barnaby wrote the note. But they are not his words. So he wrote the note and he didn't write the note. Am I understood?" she added, suddenly changing from Sherlock Holmes to Miss Witt.

"No," said Saundra.

"Gee," said Lily. "You mean it doesn't make any sense to you?" She wondered if she were wrong about the whole thing.

"'He wrote the note and he didn't write the

note,'" Saundra mimicked her. "How the hell do you expect me to understand that?"

Lily was relieved. It wasn't her problem, it was Saundra's. Sometimes Saundra was terribly thick.

"Saundra," she said, "someone *told* Barnaby what to write to you."

Saundra scoffed. "Who?" she asked belligerently.

Lily wasn't going to tell Saundra who had written the note. It would be too much for Saundra to take, coming out of the blue, just like that.

"I don't know," she said. It wasn't really a lie. She didn't know for sure, even though she was sure she knew.

"I doubt it was his mother," said Saundra.

"Oh, me too," said Lily, who found it amusing to think that Barnaby's mother might have sat him down and told him what to write.

"I mean," Saundra went on, "I've never met his mother. So why would she make him say such mean things to me?"

"But it wasn't his mother, Saundra."

"How do you know?"

"But you just said you doubted it was his mother," Lily reminded her.

"I know. But the more I think about it, the more I think it was her."

"That's ridiculous. It wasn't his mother, Saundra. His mother did not sit him down and tell him what—"

"Then *who*? Who was it?"

"It was a rival," said Lily.

"A rival? What do you mean, a rival? What kind of rival?"

"A rival for his affections."

"You mean—"

"Yes." Lily answered Saundra's question before she'd even asked it.

But Saundra asked it anyway: "He has someone *else*?" Saundra was staring at her, as if she couldn't believe that this might be so.

"Yes."

"I don't believe you."

"It's true," said Lily.

"How do you know? You met him only once. How do you know?"

She couldn't tell Saundra that she'd met him not once but twice: in the dressing room, when he had given her the note, and then on the stairway, when he had given her not a note but at least a message, and the message said that he was very big on kissing.

"I just know," she said.

"Well, I don't believe you. You're telling me that he has someone else, and this someone else told him to write those terrible things to me? That's ridiculous. Who would be so . . ."

Lily saw Saundra come all by herself to an understanding of the whole thing. This understanding passed over her face from bottom to top, starting with her lower lip, which began to tremble, and ending with her forehead, which became furrowed with believing disbelief.

Lily just nodded.

No tears came to Saundra's eyes this time,

but she seemed to be crying just the same. Her body shook and her teeth chattered.

"That b-b-b-bitch," she said. "What am I going to do? Tell me, Lily. What? Everything I want, she wants too. And she scares me. You know that. She's almost prettier than I am. And she's a better dancer. She is. She's a terrible person. But she's better at everything. I don't have a chance. It's just like the audition. If it hadn't been for you, I never would have won the audition. But that was just dancing. This is . . . this is . . . *love*. There's nothing we can do. She's stolen my Barnaby away from me, even before he knew he was mine. She's stolen my Barnaby away from me, even before I could show him that I would be his. . . . I mean, we never even . . . we never even . . ."

"Kissed on a stairway?"

"We never even held hands," Saundra admitted. "He never knew how much I loved him."

"From afar."

"From afar," Saundra agreed. "And now there's nothing we can do. Is there? Is there anything we can do, Lily?"

Lily knew Saundra meant whether there was anything *she* could do, and Lily simply answered, "Yes."

"Oh, thank you, Lily, thank you." Saundra threw herself into her sister's arms. "Thank you so much. I knew you'd help me. I knew it." Then she looked right at Lily and asked, "What? What can you do? He wrote me such a terrible note. What can you do? He hates me."

"I told you. The note is a mixed message. The

terrible part comes from Meredith Meredith. But I'll bet the 'Love, Barnaby' part doesn't."

"Oh, yes it does," said Saundra. "She made him put that in just to taunt me."

"No." Lily shook her head. "No, she didn't. When he gave me the note, Meredith Meredith was looking right at him. So he snuck it to me. He did. He didn't want her to see. If the note had said only what she wanted it to say, then he wouldn't have had to sneak it. But the 'Love, Barnaby' part was his part. He didn't want her to see it. He likes you, too, and he doesn't want her to know."

"What do you mean, 'too'? Maybe he doesn't like her at all. Maybe he likes *only* me."

Love was strange, Lily thought. Saundra had gone from hopelessness to craziness in less than a minute. And this was a hard one to explain. It was one thing to tell Saundra that Meredith Meredith had been there when Barnaby had given her the note. But she couldn't possibly tell Saundra about the kissing in the stairway. Barnaby might like Saundra, but Lily had seen with her own two eyes that he liked Meredith Meredith, too. It couldn't be denied, though she would have liked to say it wasn't so. But boys were strange, too. They seemed to be able to write "Love, Barnaby" to one girl and to kiss the lips of another girl, and it didn't bother them at all. They probably thought it was the most fun in the world. What a mystery they were!

"I'm sure he likes you," Lily said gently.

"But what about her?"

"Don't worry about her. I'll take care of her."

Saundra looked as if Lily had just told her she'd won the lottery. Even her gleaming white teeth, behind the smile that jumped onto her lips, seemed grateful.

"Oh, I knew you would, Lily. I just knew it." Saundra hugged her. "How?" she asked. "How are you going to do it? Are you going to intimidate her again, like last time?"

"Oh, gosh, I hope not," said Lily, as she realized that she didn't have the least idea how she was going to get rid of Meredith Meredith and make Barnaby love Saundra, all at the same time.

18

Crushed

Lily decided to ask her father his advice. From the way he'd dropped the ball into her court, she wasn't sure he was an authority on love. At the same time, he had loved her mother for over fifteen years, so he certainly had a lot of experience. Of course, his experience had been of the easy kind: he loved the Judge, and the Judge loved him, and they both knew it.

One night that week she interrupted her father as he was sitting in the spare room working on some things from the office. He was in a bad mood because he never liked to bring work home from the office. He always went around saying that he never took the office home with him. It was the same as when the Judge said that her home was not a courtroom. Both of them believed in keeping the home as a family place and not conducting their business in it. Business was fine in its own place, they said, but if you let it into your home, pretty soon it took over, and you spent your evenings with papers instead of with each other and with your children. And that was bad. You had to prefer to hold someone's hand instead of a pen or pencil; you had to prefer to look into someone's eyes instead of into a bunch of written words. Otherwise you forgot the important things in life. The fact that he wasn't getting much accomplished made his bad mood even worse.

"What are you doing here?" he growled at Lily when she interrupted him.

"I have to ask you a question."

"Can't you see I'm working?"

"I can see you were staring off into space. That doesn't look like working to me."

"Aren't I allowed to think? Don't you know that thinking is part of working?"

"Sure I do," Lily replied. "What were you thinking about?"

"None of your business," he said.

"Oh, maybe you were having dirty thoughts," she said.

"Don't be ridiculous," he said. "Besides, what's a dirty thought? There are no dirty thoughts. Haven't I taught you anything? What do *you* think is a dirty thought?"

"Laundry?" she joked.

"That's not very funny," he said. "Tell me seriously. What to you is a dirty thought?"

"I don't know," she said.

"Sex?" he asked.

"What?" she questioned, to try to get some time to gain her composure.

"You heard me," he said. "Sex."

"That's what I thought you said," she replied. "And it's funny you should ask. Because that's exactly what I wanted to talk to you about."

"What?" he said. He looked surprised and started to chew on a pencil.

"Take it easy, Dad," she said. "It's not about me; it's about Saundra."

"Oh, well in that case . . ." he said and chewed even harder on the pencil.

"What's so bad about sex?" Lily asked.

"Bad? Who said anything was bad?" He had stopped chewing on the pencil, but now he had his eyes closed.

"Then why are you a nervous wreck?"

Opening his eyes only halfway, he said, "Because it's one thing for me to discuss the subject with you, but it's another thing for you to discuss the subject with me, to march right in here and want to talk about sex. I mean, I'm willing to discuss sex anytime—any old time, really—but what I want to know now is, what *happened*? What did Saundra *do*?" As he spoke, his eyes opened so wide that they seemed about to pull Lily right into his head. He looked both scared and eager at the same time, like someone who demands to hear the news about something but has his hands over his ears.

"I get it, Dad," Lily said. "You don't mind talking about sex, but you don't want to hear about sex."

"What do you mean, hear about it?" he asked suspiciously.

"You don't want to hear that anybody did it."

He started chewing on the pencil again. "Who do you mean, anybody? What do you mean, did it?"

"By anybody, I mean anybody. Anybody, like me or Saundra. By did it—"

"You or Saundra!"

"By did it, I mean, you know, did it. Had some sex with a boy."

"Had some sex! With a *boy*!"

"Sure," said Lily. "What do you think—with a frog?"

"A frog? Frogs turn into princes, don't they? Has my princess been fooling around with a prince? Has my girl—"

"Your princess," said Lily, referring to Saundra, whom her father often called princess, "has not been fooling around with a prince. I don't even think she's been fooling around with a frog. And that's what I think is her problem."

"Her problem is that she hasn't been fooling around with a frog?"

His eyes were twinkling. He was beginning to joke again. So Lily felt she could be more direct with him.

"Saundra's problem is that she hasn't been fooling around with Barnaby."

"Good for her!" said her father.

He wasn't joking. Lily realized she'd given him too much credit.

"What's so good about it?" she said. "Meredith Meredith *has* been fooling around with him, and I'll bet that's why she can get him to do anything she wants, even to write Saundra such a nasty

121

note that Barnaby didn't want to write in the first place. Remember?"

Lily had told her parents about the note the morning after she'd learned what was in it. They hadn't known what to make of it until Lily told them it was a mixed message. They'd agreed that's what it was but still didn't know what to make of it. Lily had been thinking about it ever since and had come to the conclusion that one of Saundra's problems was that Meredith Meredith was fooling around with Barnaby and she, Saundra, wasn't. But did her father agree? He didn't seem to. And so it was beginning to seem hopeless to ask his advice.

"I remember," he said gloomily.

"So?" she asked.

"Lily," he said. "I can't accept that kind of thinking. I'm not saying you're wrong. I hadn't thought of it before, not even when you told us about the kiss on the stairway. So you may be right about what's going on between Meredith Meredith and Barnaby. You may even be right about what's not going on between Saundra and Barnaby. But I can't accept what I imagine is your conclusion. I'll bet you think that if Saundra fools around with Barnaby, then Saundra will win Barnaby and her broken heart won't be broken any longer. Am I right?"

"Sort of," she said

"Only sort of?"

"You're right," she admitted.

"I thought so," he said. "Well, let me tell you something. Parents are conservative people. I'm not denying that. Even when they don't act conservatively themselves, they tend to be conservative about their children. It's not that they want to hold their children back . . . except that it is. I have to admit it. It is. They would rather have their children miss something good than do something bad. This may not be the best attitude in the world, but it's an attitude that most parents have. And your mother and I have it too."

He looked at her as if to ask whether she understood and also whether she approved. She felt she understood, but she wasn't sure she approved, so she just stared back at him and then merely motioned for him to continue. He gazed toward the ceiling and at the same time took a big swallow, which she could see because his Adam's apple took a long trip up into his throat and then slid back down. She knew he was having trouble saying what he wanted to say, but she wasn't going to make it easy for him.

"Well, then," he began. "Anyway. Okay. Listen." Then he cleared his throat. His rehearsal made Lily impatient, but still she waited.

"So," he said. "So. Whether our attitude is good or bad, here's what it is: Saundra must not fool around with Barnaby." He closed his mouth and started to play with his pencil between his fingers.

"Is that all?" said Lily, unable to believe that he didn't have more to say.

"I think so," he said.

"Is that really all?" she asked.

"Lily," he said, "you're making this very hard for me."

"I know it," she admitted.

He smiled weakly and reached out and put

123

his hand into her curly hair. "You don't give up, do you?"

"I want to know things, Dad."

"Like what?" he asked, making a face that said he hoped she wouldn't answer.

But she had to. "Like what Saundra should do. Like what's so wrong about fooling around with Barnaby."

Now he put the other hand in her hair and pulled her toward him so that her head pressed against his chest. "Oh, Lily," he said. "I wish I knew what Saundra should do. I wish it were so simple that if she just went off and did with Barnaby whatever Meredith Meredith is doing with Barnaby, then everything would be all right. But it doesn't work that way. Believe me, there's nothing wrong with sex. Sex is terrific. But *using* sex is wrong. Maybe you can win someone by using it, but you win them that way only by losing part of yourself. And that's never a good bargain, never. I'm not saying Barnaby wouldn't be delighted if Saundra gave herself to him—I'm sure he'd jump for joy—but men are silly that way, and no matter how high they jump, when they come down to earth they tend to land on the person who made them jump for joy in the first place. And they crush her. That's what they do. They crush her." He stopped talking. His face was very sad.

"Gee," said Lily. "I wouldn't want Saundra to be crushed that way."

"Then you get my point. Neither would I."

"But, Dad."

"What is it?" He took his hands from her hair and looked right into her eyes.

"Saundra is already crushed. She *didn't* give herself to Barnaby, but she's crushed anyway. What can she do? It doesn't look as if she can win no matter what she does."

"Don't say that." He looked away. "It can't be that hopeless."

"But what can she do?"

"What can *you* do?"

"Me?"

"Do you know why your mother and I have left so much of this in your hands?"

"Sure," said Lily. "You guys don't know how to handle it yourselves."

He laughed. "That isn't what I was going to say. But I can't deny it, either. We were nervous about it right from the beginning. And to tell you the truth, it's always been hard to communicate with Saundra. In fact, it's been impossible. We used to be afraid that no one was going to be able to make her come out of herself. She's a very talented person, your sister, but she's never trusted her talent or believed in herself. Only you have been able to make her do that."

"Yeah, because she knows she's better than I am."

He touched her head again. "No. Because she hopes to be as good as you are."

"Yeah. I'm some dancer," said Lily, because it was easier to make fun of herself than to start prancing around the room trying to pretend her sister really looked up to her.

"No," he said. "But you're some kind of sister."

"And what else am I?"

He guessed, putting his finger to his chin to

help him concentrate. "You're the great detective of love. You're going to solve the mystery of how Saundra can win her prince."

"Including no sex with a frog."

He tried not to laugh but he couldn't stop himself. "Right. Including no sex with a frog."

"But you still didn't get it right." She opened her arms before him. "What else am I?"

He got it right this time. "You're some kind of daughter!" And his arms flew open too.

19
Dancers on the Floor

First she decided she would give Barnaby the autograph that Meredith Meredith had given her. "I HATE YOUR GUTS," it said and was signed, "Meredith Meredith." That would break them up for sure. Barnaby would go crazy. He would never speak to Meredith Meredith again as long as he lived. He would wipe her from his memory for all eternity.

But would that make him love Saundra? Or would he turn against all women, after being betrayed so heartlessly by one?

Besides, it wasn't honest. Meredith Meredith hadn't written the autograph for Barnaby. She'd written it for Lily, and then she'd told Lily to give it to Saundra. It was for both of them, the sisters love-tangled, but it wasn't for Barnaby. Anyway, since when had she let someone else write her notes for her? The last thing she needed was Meredith Meredith as a ghostwriter.

So she decided to write Barnaby a note of her own. The problem was how to get it to him. She could try to find out where he kept his street clothes and slip it into one of his pockets while he was in class or at rehearsal. But how did she know then that he'd ever see it? Maybe he was one of those people who at the end of the day threw out everything in their pockets but their change and tokens, in order to feel they would get a fresh start in the morning and have no debts left over from the day before. Or maybe he would find the note and resent the fact that she'd gone through his clothes without his permission, and he'd ignore it or send it back to her with "mind your own business" written all over it.

The only thing she really knew about him was that he rehearsed in the same room as Saundra and Meredith Meredith, way up on the sixth floor. It was going to be very hard for her to sneak up there and hand him a note without Saundra and Meredith Meredith seeing her.

But that was it! There was one sure way of getting the note to him. She would give it to Meredith Meredith to give to him! It couldn't fail. Or maybe it could. But if it did, then everything would be ruined. And if everything were ruined then at least everything would be over. Saundra's heart would be broken completely, Lily would be to blame, so her own heart would be broken, and they would be even and could start all over from the beginning, broken hearts and all. Even tha would be better than not knowing what was going to happen and watching Saundra slowly waste away.

Lily thought of herself surrounded by a vast, swirling storm, and she thought of herself as caution, and she thought, what the heck, I'll throw caution to the winds. It sounded like such a daring thing to do. She'd always wanted to throw caution to the winds but had never known how. Now she knew.

She wrote the note after she'd changed into her dancing clothes, and then sat on the bench in the dressing room and waited. She waited until she couldn't bear it any longer and finally went up to one of the older girls, who was lying flat on a bench sweating and smoking a cigarette and apparently doing some kind of breathing exercise because she kept making her stomach rise like a balloon, and asked, "Excuse me, but do you know where Meredith Meredith is?"

It was Aurora, the girl who had flicked her cigarette at Meredith Meredith. Her parents had named her after the princess in the ballet *The Sleeping Beauty* because, as everyone in the school knew, they were big dance fans and hoped this would make their daughter want to be a dancer. Everyone also knew that Aurora hated dancing—she herself said that she hated even walking because it took too much energy—but that hadn't stopped her parents. They'd enrolled her in more ballet classes than any other kid in the school, hoping she'd change her mind and make them proud of her, but she only got worse and worse, not only as a dancer but also as a person. She was known as the laziest person in the school and also

the one with the meanest mouth, worse even than
Meredith Meredith's. But Lily couldn't help it,
she kind of liked Aurora. She felt she understood
why Aurora was so awful and thus forgave her in
advance for all her spitefulness.

"Of course I know where Meredith Meredith
is," Aurora said without opening her eyes. Smoke
came out of her mouth when she spoke. Lily imagined that the smoke turned into the very words
she was saying, so that they appeared above her as
if she were a character in a cartoon. Aurora was
easier to take this way.

"Where?" asked Lily.

"Who wants to know?"

"Oh, cut it out, Aurora. It's me. Lily."

"I heard you made a fool of Miss Witt."

"That's not—"

"I heard she loves you for it."

"I don't—"

"I think you've taught us all a great lesson in
life."

"What lesson?"

"If you want someone to love you, you have
to stand up to them first." Aurora opened her eyes
for the first time and looked right at Lily. "You
have to hurt them."

"But I didn't—"

"Yes, you did." Aurora let her cigarette hang
from her lips and took a deep breath so that her
stomach ballooned. "And I just want you to know
I'm grateful to you."

Lily couldn't understand what Aurora was talking about. That is, she understood, but she didn't
agree. It was not a good idea to humiliate anyone.

130

She changed the subject. "What are you doing with your stomach?"

Aurora had to let it deflate before she could talk. "Yoga breathing," she said. "To relax it. I have an ulcer."

"Does it hurt?" asked Lily, not quite sure what it was but knowing that it sounded awful.

"All the time."

"Are you supposed to smoke?"

"No," said Aurora, taking a deep puff on her cigarette.

"Then why are you?"

"Smoking relaxes me. The ulcer comes from not relaxing. I'm trying to cure the ulcer by being more relaxed. Get it?"

Lily nodded, though she knew Aurora was twisting things around in her own mind.

But she couldn't say this to Aurora. So she changed the subject again, back to the original one.

"Have you seen Meredith Meredith?"

Now Aurora sat up. She threw her cigarette on the floor and put it out beneath her ballet slipper. It made Lily wince to see that.

"No," she said, "I haven't seen old Double M. But I know where to find her. But if you find her, you still won't be able to see her."

"I don't get it," said Lily.

"Of course you don't get it," Aurora said, becoming her usual mean self. "You're too young to get it. So why don't you just forget the whole thing?"

"Why don't you just tell me where Meredith

Meredith is," said Lily, trying to sound like Aurora, except her voice came out too high and squeaky.

"She's hiding," Aurora said, grinning.

"Where?"

"Underneath the prince." Now she giggled.

"Who's the prince?"

"Who's the prince!" Aurora mocked her. "Barnaby. Beautiful Barnaby."

"I know Barnaby," Lily said.

Aurora laughed. "Not the way Meredith Meredith knows him."

"He is like a prince," Lily said.

"That's not what I meant," said Aurora disdainfully. "He's the prince in the ballet. In *Giselle*. Prince Albrecht. Your sister is Giselle, his lover . . . but only on stage, if you know what I mean." She laughed again. "Meredith Meredith is Myrtha, Queen of the Wilis . . . but only on stage. In real life, Meredith Meredith is the lover. The three of them make the neatest little triangle. Except it's hard to find Meredith Meredith these days because she's always underneath the prince. Just where your sister would like to be."

"First of all," said Lily, "you're wrong about Barnaby. He's Duke Albrecht, not Prince Albrecht. I read up on *Giselle*, and I know that for a fact. And secondly, my sister has no desire to be crushed underneath Barnaby, whether he's a prince or a duke."

"Crushed!" screamed Aurora. "That isn't exactly what—"

"Crushed," said Lily. "Saundra is going to make Barnaby jump for joy, but he's not going to crush her."

"Jump for joy! What are you *talking* about? Don't you know anything about sex?"

"I know everything," said Lily. "I know all about getting crushed. And Saundra—"

"Laid," said Aurora, smirking and sticking another cigarette into her mouth. As she lit it she lay back down on the bench and took a deep puff and let all the air and smoke go to her stomach, which rose up into the air. "Getting laid is not necessarily getting crushed."

"It is if you let the man land on you," Lily said, hoping she wasn't making a fool of herself.

Aurora's stomach flattened as she blew the air from her mouth. Then, with her eyes closed, she smiled. "You've got a point there," she said. "I'll have to remember that the next time some guy wants to lay me. 'You can lay me, but don't crush me,' I'll tell him. Right?"

"Right," said Lily.

" 'You can lay me, but don't crush me,' " Aurora repeated. She sat up and flung her lighted cigarette across the room. Looking up at Lily with a sad and angry face, she said, "Meredith Meredith is in the basement."

"In the basement? What's she doing in the basement?"

"Probably being flattened like a pancake by the prince. But why don't you go and find out for yourself?"

"In the basement?" Lily repeated, still unable to believe it.

"Don't say I told you so," said Aurora, whose look of anger had changed to one of pain. She clutched her stomach in her hands so that what

133

little flesh was there came out from between her fingers. "I hope you get her the way you got Miss Witt."

"But I didn't—" Lily started to protest.

"Leave me alone," said Aurora. "I've got to practice."

"What are you practicing?" asked Lily as she made sure she had the note tucked into the top of her leotard and started toward the door.

"Murder," said Aurora.

Lily went along with the joke. "Who are you going to kill?" she asked.

"Everyone but you," said Aurora.

"Gee, thanks."

Aurora laughed a crazy kind of laugh as she lit another cigarette and lay back down on the bench. "Think nothing of it," she said. "That's what I tell everybody. But the truth is, nobody's safe from me. Nobody."

She closed her eyes and blew out a stream of smoke. Her wounded stomach rose in the air. Lily looked at her and felt very sad for her and walked out of the room without saying another thing.

She'd never been to the basement before, but she figured she'd find it easily enough just by going down the stairway until she couldn't go down any farther. She passed the ground floor, with its bulletin boards announcing all kinds of events and opportunities and the security guard who never stopped anyone except to flirt, and found herself in a basement just like the kind of basement in her apartment building. There were fat pipes and thin pipes running up along where the walls and ceiling met, a constant rumbling that probably came from some kind of generator, and lots of little rooms off the many corridors.

She looked into room after room and found nobody. Just when she was about to give up and was beginning to be angry with Aurora for sending her on a wild-goose chase, she heard sounds coming from a room at the end of the last corridor she had found in the whole basement. They were sounds of moaning and groaning. As Lily approached on tiptoe, and the moaning and groaning grew louder, she imagined she was about to witness a kind of dungeon practice room to which a dancer was taken when she just couldn't seem to learn a particular step or move or series of steps or moves and was forced to do it over and over until she moaned from the pain and exhaustion and still was made to practice and practice and was not released until she'd mastered what had seemed before impossible for her body to do or she had fallen senseless to the floor.

When she looked into the room, she saw two dancers on the floor. But they were so wrapped up in each other, their naked bodies were so intertwined, that they seemed to be only one.

They were very beautiful. They were sweating like statues made of real flesh, and they moaned as they breathed, and their breathing made their bodies rise and fall. Their eyes were closed and their mouths were open and his hands fit around her waist as if he would never let her go and her legs were clasped around his legs, and Lily thought how much this was like a dance. It was a dance. It was a dance of love. And she felt she could watch it forever.

She got the chills, the way she did when she watched her sister dance on the stage and do something glorious that Lily never knew Saundra could do. She felt like applauding now, as she did then, no matter that it wasn't the right time to applaud, that someone was dying on the stage or two people were making love on the floor.

But she did nothing to interrupt them. She watched, and saw how beautiful and clean and sweet and nice it all looked, and she thought of her parents making love on Saturday afternoons, perhaps at this very moment, and then she thought of Saundra, who probably wished she were down here in the basement on the floor with Barnaby instead of Meredith Meredith.

Poor Saundra. If anything would crush her, it would not be doing this but not doing this and knowing it was being done.

Lily turned away from the two dancers loving on the floor. She had to find Saundra. She didn't know what she was going to tell her, but she had to find her.

She ran out of the basement and up the stairs and all the way to the sixth-floor rehearsal room, where she imagined everyone would be shaking their heads over the absence of Barnaby and Meredith Meredith.

But the room was empty, vast and quiet and rather ugly, she now saw, with no movement in its air. It was also lonely. "Saundra," she called, thinking that her sister might be hiding in one of its corners, because her sister was lonely and empty too, and the top floor of the building was as far as you could get from the basement, and Lily felt that somehow Saundra must be able to feel what was going on down there. It was one thing for Saundra not to have known about the kissing on the stairway, even though it had been happening just a few yards away from where she'd been standing. But it was another thing not to know about a naked embrace. Lily imagined that if you loved someone, and he was naked and embracing someone naked even halfway around the world, you would know it, you would feel it.

"Saundra," she called again, loudly enough this time for the name to echo and come back to her, so it was as, if she herself were Saundra and she was looking for herself. Well, she was Saundra in a way. They were sisters. And one of them, Lily discovered after she had searched through the whole school except for the basement, was missing.

20

L-o-v-e
o-n
t-h-e
F-l-o-o-r

She asked around and found out that Saundra's rehearsal had been cut short because no one could find Duke Albrecht and Myrtha, Queen of the Wilis. When Lily heard that, she said simply, "How crushing." Then, deciding to skip her own class entirely, she raced home to find Saundra.

The number 10 bus on Central Park West was nowhere in sight, as usual, so she ran the more than twenty blocks. She hadn't even bothered to remove her tights and leotard and had simply slipped on her jeans and put her sweat shirt into her dance bag. Of course she'd changed her dance slippers for her trusty Adidases, so she felt she was really flying home the way her father used to fly around the reservoir before he'd given up running in order to ride his stationary bicycle in order to get nowhere fast.

It wasn't until she'd pushed through the front door and called out, "Anybody home? Saundra?" that she realized the note was still stuck in the top of her leotard.

She removed it and was looking at what she'd written on the outside—FOR BARNABY, HIS EYES ONLY—when her father appeared at the end of the hall that led to the bedrooms. He had on his bathrobe and his hair was a mess.

"What are you doing home so early?" he asked. It didn't sound as if he was glad to see her.

"Looking for Saundra."

"She's at rehearsal. And you're supposed to be at class. Do you realize what time it is?"

"Dad, that's what you're supposed to say when someone's late, not when they're early. Besides—"

"There are times, young lady, when it is as upsetting for someone to be early as it is for her to be late. *More* upsetting."

"But—"

"Now you march right out of here and go back where you came from." He pointed toward the front door and turned and started to walk back down the hallway to his bedroom.

"But, Dad, Saundra's missing."

"What?" came his voice.

"Saundra's missing. She was supposed to be—"

"What?" he said again, but now he was rushing toward her and reached out and put his arms around her as if to make sure that *she* wasn't missing.

"She was supposed to be at rehearsal, but the rehearsal ended early because . . . well, never mind why, but the rehearsal ended early, and

139

Saundra . . . I looked for her everywhere, but she
. . . she just disappeared."

"And what's this?" he said, his voice frantic,
as he pulled the note from her hand. "Did she
leave you a note? Or . . . is this from a kidnapper?"

He didn't read the outside or wait for her to
explain. He just pulled it open and moved his eyes
down the words. Once, twice, three times he read
the note. Then he read it aloud: " 'Dear Barnaby.
You may be jumping for joy, but if you really want
to know the truth, you're the one who's being
crushed, and the crusher is a beautiful ballerina.
Your true love is a beautiful ballerina also. If you
want to solve this mystery, meet me in the same
place as before. Your friend, the Chipmunk, who
is not studying to be an actor but a writer, as you
can probably tell.' "

When her father stopped reading, his mouth
kept moving. He must either have wished such a
terrific note would go on longer or he was flabber-
gasted.

To help him make up his mind, Lily said,
"Pretty good note, huh, Dad?"

"What does this mean, Lily?" He was shaking
the note like a fan, but the way he did it made it
seem as if he'd like the note to fly off into space or
catch on fire.

"That's just the point, Dad. I'm the only one who
can explain it. It's really for Barnaby. But it's also for
Meredith Meredith. I was going to give it to her—"

"What does it *mean*, Lily?" he asked again

"I'll get to that, I'll get to that," she said, all
excited at finally being able to explain her brilliant
plan. "See, I was going to give it to Meredith

Meredith to give to Barnaby. It has his name on it, after all, and it says that he's the only one who's supposed to read it. So—"

"Yes, so? How can it be for her if—"

"Exactly! I knew, I just *knew* that if I said it was for his eyes only, she'd be sure to read it before she gave it to him. But then I made it so mysterious that—"

"I'll say it's mysterious. Lily—"

"Right! I made it so mysterious that she'd *never* understand it. She'd know it was about her—believe me, if there's anyone who thinks she's a beautiful ballerina, it's Meredith Meredith—but she wouldn't know if she was the crusher beautiful ballerina or the true-love beautiful ballerina. So she'd show it to Barnaby for him to explain it to her. And then he'd read it and he'd meet me at the bench in the girls' dressing room and—"

"The girls' dressing room!"

"Oh, Dad, that's okay. Don't worry about that. Boys often come into—"

"And the Chipmunk? Need I ask who is this Chipmunk?"

Lily beamed proudly, both for herself and for her father. They were both so smart. And if he could figure out that she was the Chipmunk, then Barnaby would certainly know. After all, she and Barnaby had discussed chipmunks; chipmunks were maybe the only thing she and that gorgeous hunk had in common, except they both loved Saundra, even if Barnaby didn't know he loved Saundra.

"All right, Chipmunk," her father said. "Let me get this straight. Not about the note, I mean. About Saundra. What you're telling me is—"

Lily heard her mother's calling voice interrupt him: "Harold, what's keeping you? Is someone there?"

He grabbed Lily's hand. "Come on," he said. "I think your mother should hear this." He started to pull her down the hallway toward the bedroom. "Judge, are you decent? Cover up. I've got Lily with me."

He was in such a hurry, obviously in concern over the missing Saundra, that they reached the bedroom just as Judge Leonard was diving under the bedcovers. Lily could tell that her mother didn't have on a stitch. And as her father almost pushed her onto the bed and sat down beside her, Lily got the feeling that everywhere she turned, on a Saturday afternoon in the middle of summer, with the sun still above the tops of the trees and the air as warm as your breath, she was surrounded by naked people having the time of their lives making love. She was catching them at it right and left. It made her feel happy and sad at the same time: happy to see other people happy; sad to see herself only seeing them, not being them. But she promised herself that someday she'd be just like them, except maybe she'd lock the door so some snoopy detective like herself couldn't come along and get such mixed feelings over what she was witnessing.

The Judge was lying there with the covers up nearly to her nose, trying to say something to Lily but able only to blink and smile. Lily felt she knew her mother well enough to know that she wasn't doing this because she was embarrassed at being discovered in the middle of her usual Saturday playtime but because she was angry that she'd been interrupted yet knew that her anger wasn't really right—it wasn't Lily's *fault*, exactly—and so tried to conquer her anger with a smile and a few words that would probably be something like, "Hello, there, early bird," if she could only get them out.

But before Lily's mother could really say anything, her father said, "Now just stay calm, Judge, because there's probably nothing to it, but Saundra's missing."

The Judge sat up so fast she nearly lost her covers and said, "What! Missing! What are you—"

Lily's father, who had been just as frantic when Lily had told him the news, now spoke calmly. He always seemed to get calm when his wife got upset. It was as if they had a kind of scale and spent their whole lives balancing on it. "Now just take it easy," he said. "I'm sure there's a simple explanation. And Lily's got it, I'm sure of that, too. Right, Lily? And please refrain from reading us that note. Just tell us—"

"Note!" the Judge nearly screamed. "What note? Has Saundra been kidnapped? Are they asking for a ransom? I must see that note. You have no right to keep it from me. I—"

"I'm sorry I mentioned it," her father said. "Believe me, the note has nothing to do with this."

"Stop hiding things from me," said the Judge. "I insist!" And she held out her hand.

Lily gave her the note. The Judge read it and then read it again. Lily couldn't help feeling proud. If the note so baffled her brilliant parents, it would absolutely have driven crazy the dumb Meredith Meredith.

"This is your handwriting. So I take it you're the Chipmunk. Am I right?" said her mother, with her eyes still on the note.

Lily nodded.

Her mother wasn't frantic any longer. She was very calm, almost too calm, and stern too. Lily imagined this was the way she was when she presided in court. Judge Forget-Me-Not was her nickname, because she never forgot anything. Lily bet any criminal who had seen her this way—so stern and demanding—wouldn't forget her either. Lily smiled.

"What's so funny, young lady?" said the Judge.

"I was just thinking how glad I am that your home is not a courtroom. At least not most of the time."

"Never," said her mother. "My home is never a courtroom. But that doesn't preclude interrogation."

Wow, this judge could be so tough you couldn't even understand her. "You said it!" said Lily.

"This note, I take it," said her mother, "has nothing to do with the fact that Saundra's missing." From the way her mother said it, Lily could tell that she was trying very hard not to panic; her voice was flat and empty. Lily wanted to tell her not to worry, that they were both exaggerating the situation: just because someone wasn't either home or at dancing school didn't mean she was in danger.

First, though, she felt she should answer the question. "It doesn't *really* have anything to do with the fact that Saundra's . . . not here."

"Where is she, then?" asked her mother.

Lily had to admit she didn't know.

"And the note?" her mother asked her again. "I suspect it is not entirely unconnected to this case."

"You're beginning to sound like a detective, Judge," said Lily's father.

Lily butted in quickly so everyone would know just who really was the detective in the family. "The note is not entirely unconnected to this case."

"It isn't?" said her mother, who didn't seem able to believe it though she had said it first herself. Again she seemed like a mom and not a judge. Lily's note apparently had everyone befuddled. Too bad she never got a chance to use it on the right people.

"Maybe Saundra read the note and decided to run away from home," her father said. "Maybe she couldn't stand the idea of having a sister who is a chipmunk and writes mysterious messages."

"Harold, you're not taking this serously," his wife said.

"The more I think about it, the less worried I am about Saundra . . . and the more worried I am about Lily. Saundra isn't really missing, I suspect; she's just absent. But Lily . . . Lily is writing strange notes that are addressed to one person, are supposed to be read by another person who will give the note to the first person, and they're both supposed to believe that the note in question has been written by an aspiring author who's a chipmunk." He shook his head. "No," he said, "I'm not really worried about Saundra. Saundra is fifteen years old and is probably off buying a pair of million-dollar jeans that will be so tight they'll make her look as if her skin's been painted blue by someone who's signed his name right on her behind. But I am worried about my other daughter, who has been trying to help her sister and in the process has turned into someone named the Chipmunk and has given up dancing for writing crazy messages and ends up not helping anyone at all but making matters worse because no one can understand a single thing she's doing."

Lily was hurt by this. She could understand that in fact her father *was* worried about Saundra, no matter that he was pretending not to be any longer. But there was no need for him to criticize her. They'd asked her to help mend Saundra's broken heart. It wasn't her fault if they couldn't understand *how* she was helping, and how difficult it was when all the evidence pointed to the fact that Barnaby was crazy about Meredith Meredith and didn't have anything left over to give Saundra but a mixed message.

She decided she'd better tell her parents about what she'd seen in the basement of the American Ballet Center. But first she said, "Just because you don't understand what I'm doing doesn't mean that what I'm doing is wrong. Maybe *you're* wrong for not understanding. Smart kids are not stupid because they're smarter than their parents. And if I call myself the Chipmunk, then I have a very good reason, and—"

"Lily!" her mother said, and Lily knew that she was about to be accused of what her mother called impertinence.

Lily's father put his hand on his wife's naked

shoulder. "She's right, Judge," he said. "Lily's right. We have no right to criticize something merely because it's beyond us. And, believe me, whatever Lily's up to in all this, it certainly is beyond us. But perhaps she'll explain so we can try to understand. Chipmunk?" He put his other hand on Lily's shoulder. "If you don't mind cluing us in . . ."

Lily raised her shoulder so it would fit even better into her father's hand and so he would know she still felt close to him despite the fact that he'd said things that had hurt her.

"Well," she began, "this afternoon, when I was trying to find Meredith Meredith in order to give her the note and kill about five birds with one stone, because Meredith Meredith would read the note, then she would give it to Barnaby, then Meredith Meredith would come to find me and I'd intimidate her, and Barnaby would come to find me and I'd make him want Saundra, and then he would find Saundra and they'd live happily ever after. . . . Anyway, when I had written the note and was looking for her to give it to her, someone told me where I could find her, and when I found her . . ."

Lily stopped. She just couldn't figure out how to put it into words that her parents would understand and still not think that she should be taken off the case of Saundra's broken heart because Meredith Meredith and Barnaby were doing something that Lily shouldn't see them doing on the floor in a tiny room in the basement.

"Go on," said Lily's mother. "And when you found her . . ."

It was now or never.

"She was a human pancake," Lily said.

"A what?" her parents said together.

"A flapjack."

"A *what*?" Now only her father could speak. Her mother tried, but no sound came out.

Lily took a deep breath and swallowed. If only parents could understand things when you described them without saying exactly what they were. Sometimes parents were just like babies. You had to . . . But that gave her a brilliant idea. Just the way parents did when there were little kids around and the parents didn't want them to understand something, Lily would do because her parents were around and they didn't understand even when she wanted them to and had told them as much as she could tell them without their possibly putting their hands over their ears and telling her to stop and taking her off the case. She would spell it for them.

So she took another deep breath and another swallow and began. "T-h-e-y w-e-r-e l-y-i-n-g o-n t-h-e f-l-o-o-r a-n-d m-a-k-i-n-g—"

"Love!"

A voice came from outside the bedroom door. It took the letters right out of Lily's mouth and made them into the word. "Love!" it repeated. And then it said the whole thing: "They were lying on the floor and making love."

As it said that, the voice came into the room, attached to the person it belonged to.

"Oh, my God!" said Lily's mother.

"Oh, my God!" said Lily's father.

"Yikes!" said Lily.

If it wasn't for her old pair of million-dollar jeans, they never would have recognized her.

Lily's parents had a new daughter.

Lily had a new sister.

Saundra had a new hairdo.

21

Boys

The Judge wasn't a judge, at least for the moment; she was pure Mother: "Saundra, what *have* you done to your hair?" she wailed.

"What hair?" said their father. "That isn't hair. That's . . . that's . . . that's . . ." He might as well have been looking for the word to describe a creature from outer space.

"Oh, Saundra," was all Lily could say, though she said it more than once. "Oh, Saundra."

Lily's feelings were completely mixed. She was flattered by Saundra's new hairdo, she was hurt because her father found it indescribable and her mother questionable, and she was shocked to see how awful it looked on Saundra.

"I've had a permanent," said Saundra, as if it were news.

"It's permanent?" said their father. "Heaven help us."

"Not permanent," said Saundra. "A permanent."

"You've had a permanent that's not a permanent?"

"It's a permanent, Dad," said Lily, in case he actually was confused, which she doubted. She guessed he was really just playing with the word *permanent* in order to give himself some time to think up something else to say.

"If you don't mind my saying so," their mother said to Saundra, "what it really looks as if you've had is a head transplant."

"Oh, Judge," said their father, chuckling despite himself.

"Mom!" said Saundra, looking hurt and angry at the same time. "Everyone at Kurl Korner said I looked just divine. And—"

"Where?" her mother interrupted.

"Kurl Korner," Saundra repeated. "And to tell you the truth, I wish I *could* have gotten a head transplant. I wish I could have gotten a body transplant. I wish I could have gotten a *person* transplant."

"But, princess—" their father began, still trying to find the right thing to say.

"And just what do you mean by that?" their mother asked Saundra. "That's a terrible thing to say. You're just a fine person. You have no reason in the world to wish for a transplant of any kind. You have no reason to have done even what you have done to your beautiful hair."

"Oh, yes I do!" said Saundra, her voice cracking. Lily could tell she was near tears. "Oh, yes I really do!"

"It's all right, Saundra," said Lily, reaching out for her sister's hand. Saundra didn't give her hand to Lily, but Lily took it anyway. "I understand," she said to her parents.

"Thank goodness," said her father, who seemed genuinely grateful that she might understand and for finally having something to say. "Tell us what's going on here. We'd really like to know."

"Is it all right?" Lily asked Saundra's permission.

Saundra took her hand from Lily's and pretended not to care. "How should I know?" she said. "Judging from the reception I'm getting around here, I doubt anyone understands. No one's ever understood me, anyway."

"Oh, but, darling—" their mother started to object.

"You *are* very hard to understand," said Lily. "That's true. You're a complicated person. You're an artist. All artists are hard to understand. But that's one of the things that makes them artists. They know they're hard to understand, but they really want people to understand them, and so they—"

"Get haircuts?" their father interrupted.

"It's not a haircut!" Saundra objected. "It's a permanent."

"Oh, sorry," said their father. "I guess I don't understand. Lily." He gestured for her to continue.

"Well," she began, "people want curly hair. Everywhere I go, they're trying to look like me. Or at least they're trying to make their heads look like my head."

"And you used to hate your hair so much," said her mother.

"I know," said Lily. "I felt so different. It's hard to be a little kid and feel so different. But now that I'm a big kid, I kind of enjoy feeling different . . . and look what's happening," she went on, pointing at her own, natural curly hair, "I'm beginning to look the same as everyone else."

"But that's only on the outside," said her father. "On the inside, you're one of the most different people in the world."

"I'm afraid I must agree with that," said her mother.

"Why 'afraid'?" asked her father.

"Because it's never easy to be different," her mother answered.

"Oh, I really do enjoy it," Lily said.

"Hey," said Saundra, "I thought we were supposed to be talking about me. How come we always end up talking about *her*?" And she pointed at Lily with both her finger and her haughty chin, which Lily had to admit didn't look quite so scary surrounded by a cascade of flowing black ringlets.

"But we are talking about you," said Lily. "You and I are very much the same in that way. We're both different. Maybe not different in the same way. Different in different ways. But different from everybody else as much as we're different from each other."

"Huh?" said Saundra, shaking her head.

"I understand what Lily's saying," said their father. "Lily means you're both special. Not just different. Special."

Saundra almost managed a smile and said to Lily, "You're special, too."

"See," said Lily, "we're different and we're

153

special. The thing is, Saundra . . ." She wasn't sure how to say this. "The thing is, by getting your hair curled, you stopped being so special. Because curly hair just isn't that special any—"

Saundra interrupted her by nearly screaming, "I'm tired of being special! I don't want to be special! Being special doesn't get me anywhere! Being special—"

"Doesn't get you anywhere?" said their father. "I should have thought—"

"Doesn't get me anywhere!" Saundra repeated. "Not anywhere. Nowhere. I don't want to be different. I want to be the same. So I can get what everyone else gets and have what everyone else has and do what everyone else does and be happy the way everyone else—"

"But not everyone else is happy," their mother objected. "Most people—"

"I think I know what Saundra means," said Lily.

"What?" asked her parents together.

Lily looked at Saundra. She figured Saundra knew what she was going to say and she didn't want to say it unless Saundra indicated that it was all right. But Saundra just looked at her expectantly, as her parents were doing also. Lily was on her own, as usual.

"Saundra wants to lie on the floor making love."

"What!" said her father.

"Lily Leonard!" said her mother.

"Right!" hollered Saundra.

"I knew it!" said Lily.

"Right right right right right!" said Saundra.

"That's exactly what I want to do. Just like everybody else. Just like all the other kids. But not me. Not snotty pretty Saundra. Snotty pretty Saundra doesn't lie on the floor making love. Oh, no. She just *falls* in love and then watches the worst bitch in creation come along and steal the man she loves. And how does she steal him? She steals him by—"

"Don't say it," said their mother.

"—lying down on the floor with him—" continued Saundra.

"—and making love," Lily chimed in.

"And making love," repeated Saundra. "Right, Lily. And making love. It was Lily who first told me about Meredith Meredith. What a dummy I was. I had no idea. But Lily knew. I couldn't figure out the note I got from Barnaby, it didn't make any sense. But Lily knew what was going on. She even knew that Meredith Meredith told Barnaby what to say in the note. The only thing she didn't know was what Meredith Meredith was doing to take Barnaby away from me. She didn't know it until everybody knew it, and now everybody knows it. It was the talk of the school today. That the two of them were down in the basement making love on the floor. We couldn't even have rehearsal because nobody could find them. Or nobody wanted to find them. But everybody knew. Even you knew, didn't you, Lily? You heard it, too, didn't you?"

"Sure," said Lily, not wanting to make it more painful for Saundra, just as she had not wanted to hurt her by telling of having seen the kiss on the stairway.

"Heard it?" said her father. "She didn't just hear it. Apparently she also—"

"Dad!" said Lily, hoping to cut him off.

"What? She what?" said Saundra.

"She saw them," said their father softly, as if he were trying to swallow the words because he now realized he should have kept his mouth shut.

"*Saw* them? You saw them?" said Saundra.

Lily moved her chin up and down a tiny bit.

"What did they look like?" Saundra asked.

"Saundra, really—" began their mother.

"What did they look like, Lily?" demanded her sister.

"They were beautiful," said Lily. "It was like—"

"Lily, please!" said her mother.

"It was like a dance," said Lily.

"A dance?" said Saundra.

"A dance of love," said Lily.

"Sounds nice," said their father.

"Harold!" said their mother.

"I know how to dance," said Saundra.

"But do you know how to love?" asked their mother.

"If you're asking me if I know how to make love, then I admit I'm still a—"

"I'm not asking you whether you're a virgin. I'm asking you if you know how to love."

"How can I know if I know how to love if the person I love has been stolen away?"

"That's a very good way to know, and to learn," said their mother. "Love is not just gain. Love is also loss. You must learn how to live with both."

"Both?" said Saundra. "You mean even if I win him—"

"Sometimes it's harder to keep loving someone whom you've won and you know is yours. Sometimes it's easier to love those who don't love you in return."

Lily listened and wasn't sure she understood. "But you love Dad," she said to her mother. "And you know he's yours."

"Yes, I do know he's mine, and I do love him. But it isn't easy."

Lily was shocked to hear her mother say this. She was worried her father would be terribly hurt. But when she looked at him, she saw him looking at his wife with the most wonderful smile.

"That's putting it mildly," he said and he reached out and put his hand in the Judge's hair just the way he so often put it in Lily's hair. Lily was relieved.

"That's touching the merchandise," she said.

Her parents laughed. So did Lily. Only Saundra was unhappy.

"Are you telling me there's nothing I can do?" she said to no one in particular.

"Not at all," said their mother.

"Then what?" asked Saundra.

"No one can tell you that, darling," their mother said, leaning forward and reaching out for her older daughter with one hand while clutching the sheet to her breasts with the other. "Love between two people is between two people. No one else can help you. But remember also that no one else can hurt you. Not even someone like Meredith Meredith. She seems to be plotting against you. She seems to be trying to win Barnaby away from you. I can't tell you that she won't win him—I mean winning him truly, not merely winning him by falling onto the floor with him. But I can tell you that she won't win him by taking him away from you. If he wants you, then he wants you, and nothing she can do can stop that. And I can also tell you that nothing you can do can win him, either. You don't make people love you by doing things—either *for* them or *to* yourself." As she said this, she pointed to Saundra's new hairdo. "People love you for what you are, not for what you've done. I admit this doesn't give you much leeway. It makes life seem like a terrible gamble. But often life *is* like a terrible gamble. And all you can do is to keep playing. All you can do is to be exactly who you are and hope that those whom you love for what they are will love you for what you are."

The judge released Saundra's hand and sank back against her pillows.

Her husband looked at her with a big smile, and tears in his eyes.

"I'm married to an Ovid," he said. "A female Ovid."

"What's an Ovid?" asked Lily.

"A poet of love," said her father.

"That's what I'd like to be," said Lily.

"I thought you wanted to be a detective of love," he said.

"A poet's better," she said.

"Why?" he asked.

"It's easier. There's more leeway," she said, winking at her mother because she'd stolen her word. "You can make more mistakes."

"But you haven't made any mistakes," Saundra said. She pointed to her new hairdo. "Maybe I have. But you haven't. You've been a wonderful sister. You're always—"

"Yes, I have," said Lily. "I've made mistakes. We all have. Mom's right. I thought I could win Barnaby for you. Somehow. I thought if I wrote him a note. I thought if I talked to him. I thought if I could get Meredith Meredith to read the same note and come after me again, and I could intimidate her just the way I did last time and she would lose Barnaby and you would win him, just like with the audition. But this isn't an audition."

"No, it's not," said their mother. "And you're right. We were all wrong. All of us."

"But you were just trying to help me," said Saundra. "There can't be anything wrong with that."

"She's right," said their father.

"Of course she's right about that," said their mother. "There's nothing wrong with trying to help. But . . ." She stopped. "You tell us, Lily."

"We wanted to mend your broken heart," said Lily to Saundra. "And we couldn't. No one but you can do that. All we can do is . . ."

She stopped. She wasn't sure she was right. How could it be that a person must be all alone with her broken heart?

"What?" prompted Saundra. "All you can do is what?"

"Love you," Lily finished her sentence. "All we can do is love you."

Saundra's cry filled the room as if all her pain was leaving her, leaving her body and her mind, leaving her whole.

And tears flowed from her, cleansing her.

She threw herself onto the bed, her arms spread like a bird flying home to her family. Such strong arms. They went around her parents and her little sister and they held on for dear life.

Five minutes later, after all of them had cried and then laughed at their crying and at how good they felt for the first time since Saundra's heart had been broken, Judge and Mr. Leonard let go of their daughters and started to tickle one another.

"Cockadoodledoo," crooned their father

"If you'll excuse us," begged their mother.

"Let's get out of here," said Lily.

"Before they throw themselves on the floor," said Saundra.

They both giggled as their parents turned as red as tomatoes, and then they left the room, closing the door behind them.

"They need some privacy." Lily pulled Saundra toward the front door of the apartment.

"I can't go out like this." Saundra pointed toward her hair

"What's the matter? Are you afraid people will think we're sisters?"

"I only wish." Saundra touched Lily's curly hair. "Yours is so beautiful. So real. I look so ridiculous next to you."

"I agree," said Lily. "You do look kind of funny. And to think I always wanted hair like yours. Gee, am I glad I look the way I do."

"But where does that leave me?"

"Right next to me. Come on." And she pushed Saundra out of the apartment.

"But you said I look funny," said Saundra.

"You do. We're even. Get in the elevator."

"Even?" Saundra said as Lily pressed the button for the ground floor. "Lily, where are you taking me?"

"To solve a mystery."

"But you already solved a mystery. I feel so much better than I have in weeks."

"I know," said Lily. "But this is not your mystery, this is my mystery."

"Your mystery? What mystery?"

"Boys," said Lily.

"Boys?" said Saundra.

"Boys," said Lily, and she grabbed her sister's hand as they stepped out beneath a late-afternoon sky in which both the sun and the moon looked down on them, lighting whichever way they cared to take.

ABOUT THE AUTHOR

J. D. LANDIS was born in Springfield, Massachusetts, had his first jobs digging sewers and playing the saxophone and clarinet in a jazz band, and then graduated from Yale University in 1964. Presently the editorial director of a New York publishing house, he received the Roger Klein Award for editing in 1973. His articles and short stories have appeared in numerous publications, including *American Review*, *Works in Progress*, and *The Bennington Review*.

His other books for young readers are *The Sisters Impossible*, which was an International Reading Association Children's Choice for 1980, and *Daddy's Girl* (1984). He is presently at work on a book called *Judy the Obscure*, about a girl drummer in a rock-and-roll band, and a romance called *Girl Meets Boy*.

J. D. Landis has a fifteen-year-old daughter, Sara, and a zero-year-old son, Jacob, who was just born and is inspiring a book called *Mom Spelled Upside Down Is Wow!*

TEENAGERS FACE LIFE AND LOVE

Choose books filled with fun and adventure, discovery and disenchantment, failure and conquest, triumph and tragedy, life and love.

☐	23321	**THE KEEPER OF THE ISIS LIGHT** Monica Hughes	$2.25
☐	23556	**I WILL MAKE YOU DISAPPEAR** Carol Beach York	$2.25
☐	23916	**BELLES ON THEIR TOES** Frank Gilbreth Jr. and Ernestine Gilbreth Carey	$2.25
☐	13921	**WITH A FACE LIKE MINE . . .** Sharon L. Berman	$2.25
☐	23796	**CHRISTOPHER** Richard Koff	$2.25
☐	23844	**THE KISSIMMEE KID** Vera and Bill Cleaver	$2.25
☐	23370	**EMILY OF NEW MOON** Lucy Maud Montgomery	$3.50
☐	22540	**THE GIRL WHO WANTED A BOY** Paul Zindel	$2.25
☐	24143	**DADDY LONG LEGS** Jean Webster	$2.25
☐	20910	**IN OUR HOUSE SCOTT IS MY BROTHER** C. S. Adler	$1.95
☐	23618	**HIGH AND OUTSIDE** Linnea A. Due	$2.25
☐	24392	**HAUNTED** Judith St. George	$2.25
☐	20646	**THE LATE GREAT ME** Sandra Scoppettone	$2.25
☐	23004	**GENTLEHANDS** M. E. Kerr	$2.25
☐	24781	**WHERE THE RED FERN GROWS** Wilson Rawls	$2.75
☐	20170	**CONFESSIONS OF A TEENAGE BABOON** Paul Zindel	$2.25
☐	24565	**SUMMER OF MY GERMAN SOLDIER** Bette Greene	$2.50

Prices and availability subject to change without notice.

Buy them at your local bookstore or use this handy coupon for ordering:

Bantam Books, Inc., Dept. EDN, 414 East Golf Road, Des Plaines, Ill. 60016

Please send me the books I have checked above. I am enclosing $_____ (please add $1.25 to cover postage and handling). Send check or money order —no cash or C.O.D.'s please.

Mr/Mrs/Miss_____

Address_____

City_____ State/Zip_____

EDN—10/84

Please allow four to six weeks for delivery. This offer expires 4/85.

Life, Love and Adventure from the Teenager's View

Here are books of life, love, adventure, mystery, and suspense for every teenager's interest.

☐	24486	**THE BYTE BROTHERS RECORD A WRONGDOING #5**	$2.25
☐	24447	**THE BYTE BROTHERS COMPUTE A CLUE #4** Lois & Floyd McCoy	$2.25
☐	24421	**THE BYTE BROTHERS ENTER THE EVIDENCE #3** Lois & Floyd McCoy	$2.25
☐	24418	**THE BYTE BROTHERS INPUT AN INVESTIGATION #2** Lois & Floyd McCoy	$2.25
☐	24419	**THE BYTE BROTHERS PROGRAM A PROBLEM #1** Lois & Floyd McCoy	$2.25
☐	23918	**THE CRY OF THE SEALS** Larry Weinberg	$2.50
☐	23982	**LONG TIME BETWEEN KISSES** Sandra Scoppettone	$2.50
☐	24652	**INCREDIBLE JOURNEY** S. Burnford	$2.50
☐	20951	**DOG WHO WOULDN'T BE** F. Mowat	$2.25
☐	23624	**NEVER CRY WOLF** F. Mowat	$2.95
☐	24402	**ROLL OF THUNDER HEAR MY CRY** M. Taylor	$2.50

LIPSYTE, ZINDEL, AND BRANCATO

Select the best names, the best stories in the world of teenage books!

☐	23152	COME ALIVE AT 505 Robin Brancato	$2.25
☐	24071	THE CONTENDER Robert Lipsyte	$2.50
☐	24130	THE SUMMERBOY Robert Lipsyte	$2.25
☐	24395	THE UNDERTAKER'S GONE BANANAS Paul Zindel	$2.50
☐	22722	BLINDED BY THE LIGHT Robin Brancato	$2.25
☐	22540	THE GIRL WHO WANTED A BOY Paul Zindel	$2.25
☐	23540	THE PIGMAN Paul Zindel	$2.50
☐	24394	I NEVER LOVED YOUR MIND Paul Zindel	$2.50
☐	23975	PARDON ME, YOU'RE STEPPING ON MY EYEBALL! Paul Zindel	$2.50
☐	24393	ONE FAT SUMMER Robert Lipsyte	$2.25
☐	24396	MY DARLING, MY HAMBURGER Paul Zindel	$2.50
☐	24622	CONFESSIONS OF A TEENAGE BABOON Paul Zindel	$2.50
☐	23124	WINNING Robin Brancato	$2.25
☐	23215	SUMMER RULES Robert Lipsyte	$2.25

Prices and availability subject to change without notice.

Buy them at your local bookstore or use this handy coupon for ordering:

SPECIAL
MONEY SAVING
OFFER

Now you can have an up-to-date listing of Bantam's hundreds of titles plus take advantage of our unique and exciting bonus book offer. A special offer which gives you the opportunity to purchase a Bantam book for only 50¢. Here's how!

By ordering any five books at the regular price per order, you can also choose any other single book listed (up to a $4.95 value) for just 50¢. Some restrictions do apply, but for further details why not send for Bantam's listing of titles today!

Just send us your name and address plus 50¢ to defray the postage and handling costs.
